MASK OF THE NOBLEMAN

Curse of the Nobleman Book 1

LAURA DIAZ DE ARCE

Copyright (C) 2020 Laura Diaz de Arce

Layout design and Copyright (C) 2020 by Next Chapter

Published 2021 by Next Chapter

Edited by Elizabeth N. Love

Cover art by CoverMint

Mass Market Paperback Edition

This book is a work of fiction. Names, characters, places, and incidents are the product of the author's imagination or are used fictitiously. Any resemblance to actual events, locales, or persons, living or dead, is purely coincidental.

All rights reserved. No part of this book may be reproduced or transmitted in any form or by any means, electronic or mechanical, including photocopying, recording, or by any information storage and retrieval system, without the author's permission.

*For DJ, who is willing to support me
in too much of my foolishness.*

PROLOGUE

He is gone. I can breathe a bit as this castle loosens its limbs in his absence. We are all glad he has left for an overnight hunt. For an evening, we do not have to tiptoe around his temper. When he is here, we are all haunted by the ghost of rage. The pressure is suffocating. Sometimes, when he has found some small victory, he is still so kind, so loving. But when the turn comes, we can barely pause.

How has he turned me into this? How have I become a simpering, frightened fool? How has he turned me, *me*, into a coward afraid for my skin? How could he make *me* question my worth?

I'm making my plans to leave, but I cannot just yet. I love my son too much to go, even though every minute I spend with him puts him closer to danger. My hope is that the danger that creeps, even more violent and terrifying than his own father, will pass by. That the nightmare of my past will stay hidden from my child now.

Like clockwork, my little love comes to me as I sit at the windowsill, looking at the night-blanketed landscape. He tugs at my skirt, and I look down to see those blue eyes, my blue eyes, staring back. It shocks me. I hope that the one I fear does not see those eyes and know to whom they belong.

"Mommy! Look what Master Tochtem made me!" His bright little face is illuminated by his wild blonde hair framing his perfect cherubic cheeks. *He'll need a haircut soon*, I think, brushing a stray strand from his forehead. Then I drag my eyes from his smile to his outstretched hands.

"Oh! A little bird!"

"It's a woodpecker! I saw one today and I told Master Tochtem and he said they were his favorite! He made it with some spare block in no-time!"

I take the little sculpture from him to look closer. It's a simple thing, with a few lines to delineate feathers, but it is beautiful in its minimalism. It strikes me how much I like this little carving, but then again, I have always had a weakness for pretty things. My son has also inherited that.

"It's lovely! Where should we put it? It would look lovely in the library, don't you think?" I pick him up and put him on my lap. He's perfectly fitted to me, and I am surprised at how much I can love a child again.

His face darkens. "No, I don't want to put it in the library. I showed Marcus, and he said woodpeckers are stupid. I don't think he gets to look at it then!"

A wanton chuckle escapes my lips as I stroke back his hair. "Ok, then, we can put it in my room? Or would you like it in your room?" He turns over the little bird in his hands, pensive. I think of how much he has grown in these few short years, and how much he will grow without me in the days to come. Where I am going, he cannot come with me. The thought grips my heart as if his small palm has enclosed about it. I hold him closer.

"My room, I think. We can put it on the shelf near my bed," he says finally.

"Alright, then. Very good idea, my little bear. We'll put it there." I rub his cheek with my thumb, a gesture I've picked up from one of the washerwomen here. "Speaking of which, it is quite late, let's put you to bed."

He nods and yawns in understanding. I lift him up into my arms, eager to keep my son a babe for a little longer. I love and have loved all my children, but as my youngest, I want him to stay this way forever. "So, my little bear, what story should I tell you tonight?"

He curls his head into my shoulder as I carry him to his room down the hall. The maid smiles and mutters a soft, motherly goodnight. The people here are too kind to live in constant anxiety as they do. One of Jors' hands takes a strand of my long red hair and wraps it in his perfect little fingers. When we reach the door of his room, he looks up at me, ready to break my heart, and says, "Mommy, can you tell me about the 'Polodians' again?"

I tell him everything I remember.

CHAPTER 1

Peytra ran around her room like a dog on the hunt. She rifled through her clothes, pulling on an only mildly stained day-dress. Then she hurtled between her bed and her closet to locate her left boot. Even at this height, the air was thick with the scent of baking cinnamon, cardamon, melted sugar, and other spices, which hit her from the kitchen below. It was the day of the Spring Festival, the one annual celebration filled with events, contests, and food. However, all that depended on whether or not Peytra could be out of bed and dressed in time to make the caravan. Cursing herself for waking up late, she washed her face, scrubbing off the past night's dreaming. Peytra hurriedly brushed her hair in front of the small wall mirror, setting the thick black tresses into a braided bun on top of her head. While it was smooth and even enough for her liking, she hoped her mother wouldn't look too closely and start rattling off on its imperfections.

She jogged downstairs and was met by a throng of people. Her brothers, Thom, Lukas, and Peytire, seemed to be arguing over some such arrangement.

Nearby, her oldest brothers' wives, Evete and Muriall, chatted amongst themselves, used to their husbands' continued rehashing of their sibling squabbles. Her older sisters, Helene and Marii, were carrying and cataloging items for the festival out onto the wagons. Helene's husband, Mikael, followed the two, picking up the slack where Peytra's brothers should have been. Her mother, Gerta, came out of the kitchen, another wrapped pie to go for the festival contest.

Peytra bypassed all of this commotion and headed towards the workshop she and her father shared. It was a small, single-room structure set towards the back of their country home, connected to the main house by a barely-there overhang. The space was littered with shelves, workbenches, and a perpetual pile of wood shavings the floor that seemed to accumulate no matter how often she swept. The walls of the workshop were thin such that, in the winter, the air in that shack was just as cold as the outdoors. Only the kiln served as a source of warmth in those harsh months. Now in Spring, it was lovely and cool. The breezes eased their way through the cracks and stirred up the smell of cedar and pine. Even though Peytra was running frustratingly late, she took a moment to savor the familiar and comforting aroma. This was her most sacred space, freezing, sweltering, or just right.

Her father's creations lay haphazardly across the long sections of the various tables. Mikayel Sike was a toymaker by trade who specialized in little wooden dolls with mobile joints. What the Sike toys were really known for, however, were their quality carvings, which is what Peytra contributed. As a child, her father had taught her to carve as a hobby. She took to it with gusto and, within a few years, surpassed his skill. Peytra loved to work with her hands and moved beyond carving to clay and sculpture. Working as a father-daughter team expanded the family business into more designer toys for richer families, like porcelain dolls and indulgent dollhouse sets. Peytra relished in her talent and the pride her father and mother had of her skill. What did upset her is that no one outside her family knew of her hard work.

Ottoh, Peytra's father's business partner and good friend, had made it clear that yes, Peytra's works were lovely, but their more traditional customers would be averse to knowing that a woman had been the artist behind many of their favorite toys. Or, at very least, they would be averse to paying full price for a work with a woman-carving. Thus, no one outside her family and a few village friends knew about Peytra's talents.

That is, until today. There on her workbench at the southern corner of the workshop was her entry into the most important of the festival competitions: a free-standing carved sculpture of the goddess Fregh.

The contest specifications were to create a work of art devoted to the goddess, patron of the Spring festival. The winning piece would be displayed in the city temple's altar for the following year. Whenever Peytra visited the temple, she noted with disdain that the winners were always so toothless. To Peytra's mind, they made the goddess of love into a symbol of infantile femininity. If the winning work was a painting, it was a cacophony of glossy pastel patterns. In a statue, she was even more demure and stoic, reclining on a cloud or flower bed. This was not the goddess that Peytra wished to represent.

Instead, Peytra chose to showcase Fregh's intensity. Fregh was the goddess of love and abundance, yes, but she was also the goddess of righteous fury. She was the patron of undiluted passion, for good or ill. Among the other gods, as the stories told, Fregh was respected and feared for her conviction. In many of the tales about Fregh, she carried a basket of plenty and a ruby-tipped spear. She would bless her devotees from the basket with gifts of love and bounty, and she would pierce the hearts of her enemies with her spear. She had the ability to drive mortals to pained resolutions and madness should they displease her. All her life, Peytra had never once seen Fregh represented with her divine weapon. She was sure to rectify that in her work.

The carved sculpture, a product of much work since the early winter, was a dynamic ode to the goddess and her power. It showed Fregh pointing her spear forward while stepping on a raised cliff, her basket on the ground behind her. Peytra wanted the work to have movement, so Fregh's hair was a wild set of carefully rendered horizontal locks as if they were blowing in the wind. Her dress swooped behind her, with the ends dissolving into intricately carved flowers. Peytra had spent weeks painstakingly painting the sculpture. She had mixed the deep red paint for Fregh's spear and hair by hand, using only the most deep red pigments and extracts. That very paint had stained Peytra's hands for a full two weeks after, making it look as if her fingertips had been dipped in blood. Much to her mother's chagrin, she oddly relished the look of the deep red against her brown skin. For her, it was a small sacrifice she could make in the name of Fregh, and she hoped the goddess would repay her with a blessing for the success of the statue.

In the end, she was not only satisfied with the piece but proud. She felt that she had captured

Fregh's essence, down to the determined look she had carved into the statue's glittering blue eyes.

Peytra gingerly wrapped her work up in a large sheet and headed out towards the wagons, eager to get to the festival and submit her work. She could hear through the thin walls of the workshop that her siblings and parents were almost finished readying the carts.

"Oh, well look, if it ain't the sleeping beauty. Finally get up, I see," said Lukas with a smirk. On a clear day like this, his sandy hair picked up the sunlight and almost glowed.

"Yeah, with no help from you, brother. Didn't anyone think to wake me? I could have missed the whole thing!"

"Oh, I went in there to shake you awake at dawn, and you almost bit my hand clean off!" Marii interjected, a pie held gingerly under one of her slim arms.

"Always the little beastie. Be careful, Mar, those teeth are sharp," Peytire teased.

Peytra returned her brother's joke with a few snaps of her teeth and a light punch in his arm, which he laughed off. Marii just shook her head at her younger siblings. She took out a napkin-wrapped biscuit from her pouch and handed it to Peytra.

"Here," she said, "knowing you, you probably haven't had a thing to eat yet, and you'll be picking from the pies before we even get to town." Peytra was grateful to her sister's kindness and foresight. She wondered if she could ever survive without them.

Peytire ruffled her half-falling bun as she swatted him away. "Eh, if you had eaten the pies, I wouldn't have told on yah, so long as you save me slice."

She returned his smile with a mouth full of biscuit and a shove with her shoulder. They lived across the old temple that served as their little schoolhouse for this out-lying village. It was the schoolhouse where Marii, Peytire, and Peytra had caused all sorts of mischief as children. While walking, she could see the tree nearby that they would climb and swing from.

Being the three youngest meant that they were often left to their own devices. There were no expectations on them that needed to be fulfilled that were not being met by their older siblings. Their parents, taking a more hands-off approach to parenting meant they could play and explore the world bereft of responsibilities. Even now, just a few months after her twenty-fifth birthday, she felt no pressure to do anything she did not wish to do. When women would be claiming spinsterhood or have set up some sort of venture, Peytra was content to stay on with her parents and practice her work. Or, at least, she liked to think so.

The wagons were all packed and loaded, and the large family started their journey to the city. It was just over an hour's walk away, and as they traveled, they were joined by their neighbors and other travelers, all making their pilgrimage for the festival. Peytra walked alongside the wagon, holding her sculpture. Despite the growing soreness in her shoulder, she felt the need to keep the work close and hidden. It was a clear morning, and she had a good feeling about the day. She was sure she would win the competition, and her artwork would be on display for a year. People would finally know her name, and they would commission her for carvings and statues. She wouldn't have to hide behind her father's reputation to get work. Her steps had a bounce to them the entire trek.

They reached Vergith in record time. Bright

green standards hung on the walls surrounding the small enclave, each with flowers painted on in celebration for the festival. It was impossibly crowded. This seemed to be the busiest Peytra had ever seen their little city, even compared to festivals past. Wagon after wagon jostled towards the front to be inspected and passed by the guards. This was certainly going to be the largest celebration yet.

Peytra noticed that instead of the typical two-to-four guards posted at the front there were dozens. She asked one of the younger guards, a clearly green youth who took his job much too seriously, about the added presence. The flustered boy replied that Duke Ameros had come to the festival and sent some of his personal force, and the city had put all their guard out as added protection. Indeed, she could see the bear emblem on a few of the soldiers now that she knew to look.

"Oh, so I suppose His Highness the hermit 'as come out hiding at last," Marii said in a terse whisper to her siblings so that none of the guards could hear.

"I heard," whispered Lukas to his two sisters, "that he was mauled as a youth in a strange animal attack. Now he's an unsightly mangle, so he holds up in his castle. It's a rare thing for him to be out amongst our ilk."

"I just supposed that noble people didn't really care to come out to the normal folks. And look at all this mess." Peytra indicated the traffic jam and soldiers with a jut of her chin. "It's probably best they don't come to things like this."

Marii had a quizzical look on her face. "I wonder why he'd come out now if he's all a mess. Didn't the elder Duke pass, what, six, seven, eight winters ago?

Wouldn't then have been the time to make himself known?"

"Maybe he's found a cure for his looks?" Lukas said, an impish smile dancing across his lips. Muriall scolded her husband with her eyes.

"Who cares? As long as he doesn't ruin today, he can come and go as he pleases," Peytra said, pulling her statue closer and heading towards the contest registration.

She left her name and work with the committee. Peytra swore to herself that they seemed at least a little impressed with her entry. But they wouldn't be the ones judging. It would be a selected panel of distinguished villagers and past winners. She took a tour of the competition. It was composed of three large paintings, a triptych, and another statue. Peytra felt that the competing pieces were good, at least in technique. Yet, they were all too soft and delicate for her taste. One of the paintings even had Fregh lounging among a flock of swans as flower petals seemed to stream through the air. It was pretty, but almost the same as a painting that had won two Springs prior. In fact, it seemed all of the works were rehashed versions of other winners from years before. They told the same old story about Fregh, where she was a passive, loving goddess. Peytra said a little prayer to herself, hoping that the judges would appreciate her difference.

It would be a few hours until judging commenced, so to pass the time and distract herself, Peytra decided to visit her father's shop across the city. Ottoh was there and greeted her with a warm, fatherly hug. He was a large barrel of a man with a long greying beard. It always struck Peytra as rather funny that in face and coloring, Ottoh so closely resembled her father, albeit a portly one. They could have very easily been brothers, with their laughing green eyes, bushy brows, and deep chestnut hair. But that would have been impossible, as Ottoh and his wife had emigrated from a nation in the North just before she'd been taken in by her parents.

Still, she had grown up with Ottoh acting as a self-appointed second guardian. Peytra loved him like a father, to be sure, but she also found him as annoying as any parent when he began to prescribe what she needed to be happy. "Peytra, you should smile more," "Peytra, why don't you do your hair as nice as your sisters," "Peytra, suck in your stomach," or her personal favorite, "Peytra, my little partridge, boys don't like a girl to be so challenging."

Ottoh didn't even wait until Peytra had finished saying hello before he began chastising her. "Peytra, my little partridge, look at them! Ah, you're growing so quick, when are you going to get married?" He'd probably just seen the obvious newlyweds walk by the window of the shop, their faces dumbstruck with overt affection for one another.

"But, Uncle Ottoh, if I get married, then who would take care of you, Aunt Ita, Papa, and Mama? Hmmm?" she replied with feigned sweetness.

He chortled. "No, no, my dear, no worries on that. We'll all have plenty of grandchildren to be with us in old age. But you, don't you want children? Or a man of your own to take care of?"

At this point, Peytra was inspecting their line of walking duck toys on the wall. "I'll have nieces and nephews to play with. As for a man, I'd rather take care of myself than add another to that. No, as the youngest, I'm free to be what I want."

"Ah, I always told your father you read too much. Spoiled your mind..."

Peytra was eager to change the subject. "The

store's empty today," she said. Indeed, only two browsing patrons had come in and out while Peytra was there.

"Yes! But this is fine! This year I went and set up a booth in the square where all the action is with some of the small bobbles to sell. Ita, Leahla, and Bernardo are there taking care of it. And I am here in case someone wants to come in from out of the crowd. Or saw our toys and wanted more than the booth had. See," he said, tapping a finger to his forehead, "smart!"

"Did Ita start selling her maple candies like I said she should?"

"Oh yes, we started with a small batch last week, and they sold out in two days! Today she took all of the candies she made to the booth. Wanted to see the little ones gobble them up there. That, I'll say, was a good idea, little partridge."

Peytra smiled in spite of herself. She did enjoy praise.

At that moment, while she was just noticing a small flaw in a farm set, a stranger in bright livery ran into the store and looked around. The stranger looked from Peytra to Ottoh, then ran up to the latter. Peytra noticed the bear insignia on his clothing as the page whispered hurriedly to Ottoh. Ottoh looked over at Peytra then back at the man and said loudly, "Her? She is my business partner's daughter! This is as much her store as my own. No, she is no one to worry about. His Grace is most graciously invited, and we would be honored should he deem to find us worth his presence."

The stranger ran out into the street. Peytra looked over at Ottoh, who hustled around the store already, picking up any little mess. "Peytra! Excellent news! The Duke asked for a private place, and here we are to offer it!" She answered him with a look that combined confusion with distinct annoyance.

"Don't you know what this means, girl!" Ottoh shook her shoulders. "The Duke will come in here to rest, notice our lovely toys, be impressed with yours and your father's craftsmanship, and BAM!—" he clapped for emphasis, "we'll be supplying all the toys for the royalty this side of the Gozali Mountains! Come, help me move the back table and chairs out here."

The pair rearranged the shop. Ottoh was nothing but excitement and fretfulness. Peytra just hoped this little visit wouldn't go too long and make her miss her contest. She could have tried to excuse herself but was worried that Ottoh would faint from excitement. Instead, she stood in the doorway to the back, ready to be called on should he need her help in accommodating their royal guest. In the meantime, she fretted with a seam on the side of her dress to stop thinking about the mistake on the toy she had noticed, the little sheep toy sticking out of her pocket.

Outside, there was a sudden flurry of activity as a half-dozen armored men crowded in front of the store. Five men in uniform piled into the shop, taking their places around the shelves. The Duke was personally escorted by two attendants, both in the same livery and insignia as the page from before.

Yet, it was the Duke's presence that was the most striking. He was tall, a full head taller than most men. In contrast to his brightly clothed attendants, his outfit was largely grey and black brocade. It was as if he were in mourning. He had no exposed skin, with his hands covered by black leather gloves and his head covered by a thick black hood. *No wonder he'd want to get out of the crowd*, Peytra thought, *he must be boiling in that*. But what Peytra found most frightening was the mask he wore. It was that of a bear's face, with eyes overshadowed into two narrow slits. The mask itself was a faded, white-washed stylized wooden work, lending the Duke an other-worldly appearance. Peytra looked into those slits to try and catch a glimpse of the man hidden inside. She caught a momentary flash of sky blue.

Seeing the man covered in such a way tugged at her chest in a mixture of opposing emotions. At first, she found the utter darkness and unnaturalness of his visage uncomfortable and frightening. Then she remembered her brother's explanation: that he'd been scarred and disfigured. The sympathy hit her in a thick push to her stomach, and she thought about how torn up he must have been to hide that way. To have his whole body covered to keep from the humiliation of scarred skin. She would punch that stupid smile off her brother's face for his remarks later.

"Your Grace," the attendant from before said. "Here is Ottoh Iktingard. He is the proprietor of this shop."

Ottoh performed a low, extravagant bow. "Your Grace. Thank you so much for bestowing your presence on our humble little shop."

The Duke was silent for a moment before he spoke, seeming to take in the toy store with all its distracting displays. His voice was a rich, low tenor, but not as deep nor as frightening as Peytra had assumed it would be for such an imposing presence. "No, thank you for the use of your shop. My page assured it would not be an imposition, but I am the one who remains humbly in your debt."

"No! No! Your Grace's presence here is a gift unto us! But we are glad of your favor."

Peytra hated this kind of prattling and occupied herself with rearranging the farm figures on the shelf as they went on. The Duke was seated at the small guest table, politely listening to Ottoh's continued flattery. Ottoh offered the Duke water and fruit but apologized profusely for not being able to offer wine. The Duke politely turned the food down. She noticed a tall thin guard keeping a steady eye on her. Not in a way that was lascivious but a look of wary suspicion. She could feel the guard's eyes on her hands, perhaps waiting for her to pull out a dagger from some hidden place and lunge at his master. Peytra wondered if all royalty were this paranoid.

"Is that your wife?" the Duke inquired about Peytra to Ottoh in the middle of the conversation. She realized he was referring to her, and she wanted to vomit.

"Your Grace, you flatter me to have such a young bride, but no, no, this is my business partner's daughter, Peytra. Come, Peytra." He motioned her over. "She is like a surrogate daughter to me. My wife is in the square with our son and daughters selling at the booth, so if it is possible, later I may introduce Your Grace if you are amenable."

"Business partner?"

"Yes, Your Grace. Her father is Mikayel Sike, toymaker extraordinaire and creator of all the works you see before you." Ottoh gestured to all the shelves, large sleeves billowing. Peytra knew that her contribution would be erased, but it still stung. "He is such a fine artist. Please, Your Grace, feel free to browse anything you wish."

The Duke merely tilted his masked chin in Peytra's direction. The guard who had been watching her walked over and held out his hand. In a quick second, she dared look at his eye, to see a man behind the mask, then his eyes moved back. For a frightened moment, Peytra thought that the Duke was planning on inspecting her when she looked down at her hand. In it was one of the sheep from a farming toy set she had been rearranging. It was emblematic of her father's particular brand of ingenuity, as it had a tail and head one could turn. It also had a latch in the neck so that that the sheep could open and close its mouth to make it look as though it was bleating. Peytra had spent two weeks carving the set of farm animals, but she especially loved the way she had made the "wool" look on the sets of sheep. Peytra and her father had originally toyed with the idea of using real wool but realized that it was too easy to tear or get dirty with a child's play. Instead, Peytra had carved the wood in such a way that the sheep looked like it was covered with a stylized cloud. Tiny, concentric spirals contrasted nicely with the white paint on the piece. She had devoted that same care and detail to the rest of the little sheep, down to its hooves and ears.

Handing the toy to the Duke's guard, she noticed dejectedly that one eye was slightly higher than the other. Peytra hoped he would not notice or at least not point out this mistake before she did. The Duke turned over the piece in his glove hands. He moved the head, the tail, and the mouth mechanism. Peytra wasn't sure what he thought of the toy, as his mask hid all emotion. She grew a bit anxious, hoping he wouldn't point to the mismatched eye or that he would note another distressing detail she had overlooked.

"This is quite an unusual amount of detail for just a child's toy, no?" the Duke said, again his reaction was more muted than Peytra would have liked.

"Your Grace is certainly kind," Ottoh said. "Yes, my business partner is both an innovator and a truly talented arti—"

The Duke cut him off. "How did he get the tiniest of detail on the sheep?"

"Well, in our workshop," Peytra began, Ottoh tapped Peytra's foot lightly with his, "I mean, in my father's workshop, he's rigged a large magnifier to help with the smaller details. Like a jewelry maker. And w—I mean, he uses specially designed instruments to make different depths and textures on the wood." Another small tap. "Um, Your Grace." At least he hadn't pointed out the mistake.

"But I'm sure Your Grace had fine toys growing up, I only hope our wares are agreeable to Your Grace's taste."

There was silence for a long, uncomfortable moment. Peytra had a hard time imagining this nobleman before her as a carefree child. Not simply because she couldn't see his face, but by the way his tone was measured. Even there, he gave the impression of someone who monitored their thoughts and speech to an impeccable degree. Then Peytra began to wonder at what age the Duke had been mutilated, and if he had been forced in adolescence to conceal himself. Would his injuries have healed enough for him to play? Would he have had other children to share his toys? The thought of an isolated, scared boy sent a fresh bolt of pain into her.

The Duke looked up at the guard, then towards Peytra and Ottoh. "How much for this lovely toy?"

"Oh my! You bless us with your patronage and presence! No, for His Grace's pleasure, he may have anything here gratis, in the hopes that His Grace may share them with his fine relatives and perhaps, future heirs." Ottoh smiled a salesman's smile. The prestige of noble patronage was worth its weight in gold.

"No, that's fine. I wish to support my people in all

their endeavors. Georgie, hand the man three gold pieces for the sheep."

Peytra's eyes went wide. That was more than five times what the entire set was worth. Ottoh quickly replied, "Your Grace is far, far too generous, truly ther—"

The Duke held up his hand. "It's fine. It is my duty as a lord to support my artisans in their endeavors."

With that, he got up, the guards forming around him as he politely bid them good day and left. One stayed and counted out the coin to Ottoh, who could barely contain his excitement. Peytra was stunned. All that money for one tiny sheep. At the same time, his use of "my," as in "my people" and "my artisans," made her want to punch the Duke straight through that stupid mask, scarred or no. As if he owned them.

When the last guard left, Ottoh danced around the store. He shook Peytra on the shoulders and went on and on about the type of notoriety they would have now as a toymaker, that the Duke owned one of hers and her father's creations. He was overjoyed, as he held up one coin in each hand. "This," he moved his right hand, "is for your father for making the toy, and this," he shook his left hand, "is for you, for doing such a wonderful job carving that it impressed royalty. Good job, my little partridge, I'm proud of you!" He smiled and handed her both the coins, grabbing her by the cheeks and planting a fatherly kiss on each one. She couldn't help but smile back.

The contest was quickly approaching, and Peytra rushed through the crowds of the city to get back to

MASK OF THE NOBLEMAN

the square. Her gold coin in her shift pocket felt as if it would burn a hole into her clothing. She was elated with the prospect of her own, real, individual commission. Perhaps she would buy a new set of fine tools for the workshop or put some into finer paints. Or, if she was feeling particularly reckless, she could spend it all on sweets for the rest of the year. Then she would be reminded of her hard work earnings every time she took a bite of a stuffed-bun or custard pie. She was ecstatic, but also hoped that this good fortune would last throughout the day. Perhaps it was an omen. Perhaps, she dared to dream, it was a sign she would win the contest. Peytra breathlessly, joyfully ran on, zigzagging through the crowds.

There was already a sizable crowd gathering near the main stage. The judges were talking in hushed tones among themselves at the side. She recognized a few from past years. The panel was made up of two city officials, the aging and rather boring priest from the temple, two past winners, and one artisan guild leader. Peytra looked around herself once again and noticed that the crowd somehow seemed denser than in past years. Then she noted the livery. Ah, more guards, she realized. The Duke would be crashing this as well. Perhaps this would also be good luck to her.

An announcer walked to the stage, noting there would be a delay in judging, as they would be introducing the Duke as an esteemed guest to the festivities. It seemed out of place, however, as the Duke merely gestured from his sequestered area to the side of the stage. All around Peytra, festival-goers gossiped and speculated about the Duke's appearance. Some repeated the story she had heard about his disfigurement at the claws of a bear. Some claimed it to be that he was burned by his nanny as a child, for she thought he was a changeling. Others still said they heard that his mother had thrown him into a fire in some sort of witch's ceremony and it nearly killed him. And even others whispered that his mother had been an adulterer, and thus he had paid the price by being born disfigured. Others claimed he had been cursed with the skin of a lizard to pay for his father's cruelty.

For some reason, this began to annoy Peytra. It wasn't that she was fond of the Duke — they had shared few words. But it was that now, having met him, she had an affinity for him, in the way a person may have an affinity for the storekeeper they pass on their daily walk to work. He'd become just the tiniest bit more familiar, and while something made him seem arrogant and distant to Peytra, he had not done anything to make himself particularly offensive to her yet, especially as he'd overpaid for the toy.

Except, now, the introduction had turned into a heraldic reading of his ancestry, making his presence the cause of a painfully long delay. As the minutes crept on, Peytra grew restless. She was desperate to know if she'd been judged well, and that desperation was wearing her patience and affinity thin. The herald prattled on and on with Great Marquis this and Great Duchess that, etc., and the restless crowd shared more inane prattle on the Duke's condition. Anxiously, Peytra touched her hand to her now lucky gold coin and prayed for the ceremony to begin.

The herald finished, not soon enough for anyone's liking. Not even soon enough for the Duke, who had stopped paying attention and was in conversation with one of the guards, pointing out some piece on the stage.

The judges came forward and introduced themselves. They then introduced the contestant works to the crowd, one by one. When hers was called, Peytra heard a loud set of cheers from behind her and, looking to the crowd, she made out her family gathered as a group towards the back. She smiled. It warmed her to have their support.

Finally, the announcement came. Peytra held her breath. The lead judge went forward – he was a balding man in his late forties – a set of small spectacles reflecting the simple roundness of his face. "Third place, Pollit Rovere," he shrieked. The crowd cheered for the triptych's maker. She could see Pollit ahead – he was a kind enough man, although a bit dull and uninteresting in most conversations she'd had with him in the past. He waved back at everyone as he was pulled forward and congratulated with a small ribbon and a few jars of preserves as his prize. He was smiling wide with a deep pride. *Well, good for him*, Peytra thought to herself. She was glad he'd done better than he probably expected.

The crowd went silent in their applause to hear the next name. The announcer straightened his spectacles and read from his paper.

"Second place," he squealed, "Peytra Sike."

There were sympathetic cheers, but disappointment swept over her in such a way that Peytra could not hear them. Numbly she walked to the stage, deaf now to the congratulations around her. As if under a spell, she collected her prizes, a ribbon and stretch of black velvet cloth. Perhaps it was a bit of hubris, but she had been sure that hers would win for its originality and technique.

When it came time, she looked up to see the winner: Fregh among the swans.

CHAPTER 2

It was early evening when the rain came. The Sike family was already in their homes, retired by their fires. They had recounted the adventures of the day to one another on the trek home, husbands and wives gossiping this and that. Peytra'd been uncharacteristically silent as she walked back, the goddess statue tucked under her arm, this time wrapped in the black velvet she had won. Her siblings had first congratulated her and their mother for their wins: Peytra for the statue and her mother for a first-place ribbon in a pie contest. However, it soon became clear that Peytra was not in a celebratory mood, so her brothers took to ridiculing of the winning piece and her sisters simply took turns holding her hand and tried to make her smile. Really, what would she do without them?

In Peytra's little home, it was only her and her parents, as Marii would be spending the week with Helene and her husband for a meeting with the weaver's guild, which was their trade. Peytire would be helping Thom with a new roof the next day, and the three brothers were to spend the evening drinking and generally making a ruckus.

Peytra had excused herself early in the evening to curl up into her bed and have a good long cry. She'd been holding back the tears since she'd heard the words "Second Place" but had kept them tight in her chest. It was not the prize she had wanted, nor the one she had felt she deserved. Now she laid down under her quilt listening to the sound of the thunderous rain and cried into her pillow. Somewhere in her heart, she knew that the contest didn't really mean anything. It had been mentioned that second place was excellent for a first-time contestant. This did little to quell her disappointment, frustration, and bitterness.

There was a loud knock on the door. So loud, in fact, that Peytra thought lightning had struck a nearby tree until she heard it again. She dried her eyes and ran downstairs, grabbing a spare fire poker on the way to the front door, in case she had to fight off a stray bandit. Her parents were already at the door. Her mother was armed with a wood axe, casually by her side, as Mikayel opened the front door. Standing there in the dark, soaked by the rain, was one of the Duke's pages and, behind him, a dozen soldiers.

"Good evening," the page said, bowing. "His Grace hopes you will forgive this intrusion on such an evening. However, we are in need of your assistance. His Grace's carriage and another cart have broken in the mud. Two of our guards have taken ill. Normally this would not be too much of a burden, but with this weather, it has left our Duke stranded. His Grace formally requests the use of your home for however long the storm lasts."

"Come in! You must be freezing!" Mikayel said with a gruff voice. His eyes met his wife's and communicated his thoughts silently to her. This was something they had learned from close to forty years of marriage.

"Yes! Yes, and where are the poor sick dears?" Gerta asked. "I'll start the kettle. Peytra dear, why don't you come help me in the kitchen?"

Peytra was stunned for a moment that her parents were letting strangers into their home. But then she also realized they had no choice. She followed her mother into the kitchen, only partially listening as Greta fed her warnings of not being alone with any of the Duke's men. They sliced bread and boiled water while, in the other rooms, Mikayel Sike puttered around the home, grabbing blankets and settling the soldiers. He burst into the kitchen as the tea was almost finished.

"Peytra, I need you to do something."

"Yes, Papa?"

"The Duke is insistent on sleeping separately from the others in the house and noticed the workshop. He'll be sleeping there."

"What?"

"I suspect it has something to do with the fact that he will be disrobing and wants no one to see him, except for two trusted guards at the door. He's strange, he has no attendant or valet like other royals. Those royal types always have a mess of..." and he trailed off into his old memories as a guard in his youth.

"Yes, and, Papa?"

"I need you to sneak off and go make the workshop livable before he gets there. I don't know these soldiers as men, and I don't want them making a mess of our work things. It'd be treason if the Duke just accidentally scratched himself on a stray whittling knife. Go. Hurry."

She grabbed some blankets and pillows and

went out the back. It was still pouring, but she crept as skillfully as a cat beneath the awnings, avoiding the rain as she often did in this weather. The workshop was colder than it should have been at this point in the year, even with the rain. Peytra lit all the lanterns she could, but it barely alleviated the draft. She set to work, moving hers and her father's tools to their designated homes, setting up the bedding on the large central table and putting inventory to the side. In the far corner, she could see the statue that had failed to capture first place. Her father had draped the second-place ribbon over it proudly. For a few moments, she just stared at the thing and contemplated smashing it to bits with a hammer.

Then the room turned colder as the door opened and the Duke walked in. Peytra turned around to see him there, still in his full-bodied garb, only his eyes peeking out of the discomforting mask. There was silence for a moment as both parties evaluated the situation. Peytra held tighter to the small piercing tool she had been about to put away. While she'd had her moment with him earlier, that had faded to the uncomfortable situation of being alone with a nobleman. The Duke was uncertain of how to order a girl out of a section of her own home and whether to speak first.

Peytra broke the short silence. "Your Grace," she awkwardly curtsied, "the room is almost prepared, and I'll be out of here in a moment."

"That will do, but – don't I recognize you?" He looked from her then and to the statue in the corner. He walked briskly to it for a moment and then peered back again. "Ah, yes. Now I remember. The toy shop. It was Paytree, correct?"

Her face soured. "Peytra, Your Grace."

"Ah, yes, and I remember this statue from the contest. Yours, correct?"

"Yes—"

"This one was my favorite," he turned back to her then back to the statue, his voice turning to a boyish enthusiasm. "I thought this one should have won. Truly, you really captured Fregh. That determined stare she had, down to even the way she holds her spear, with her middle finger out and—"

"You almost sound like you know her." Peytra momentarily forgot she was talking to a man that owned her and her family's livelihoods. He paused and turned back to her and tilted his head. With his mask on, Peytra had no idea whether or not this man was infuriated with her, which is what she assumed. "I mean, I'm sorry for interrupting Your Grace, umm. I just mean."

"No. No. It's fine. I'm just not quite used to it. Talking to an unfamiliar subject like this, it's, it's new."

"Really?" She chafed at the word "subject."

"Well, yes."

"Well, it's weird for me. You're the first noble I've ever really talked to."

"I take it you never had to meet with my father then?"

"No, not really. I mean, my dad used to work as a guard for your father in his youth. But that was long before I was born."

"Ah, and the owner of this home is your father then? And his wife your mother, then?"

"Yes. Of course." Peytra knew what was coming.

"It's just intriguing because, you know, you really look nothing like them. You are so," he paused, "warm."

She pursed her lips at the comment she had

gotten her entire life. "Yes, well. My mother's family is from a nation in the Southeast. All my siblings too after our father, but I look like my mother's kin.""

It finally dawned on the Duke that he had made a faux pas. "I'm sorry I said that. I didn't mean to—"

Peytra didn't care about interrupting anymore. "It's fine. It happens all the time."

"Yes, but I shouldn't have just assumed otherwise." Something in the way that he changed his stance or moved his head told Peytra that he was sincere.

"Anyway. I did want to meet you because I realized that the artist behind this statue and the sheep doll was one and the same. I'm horrible with names and thought, at first, it was your father. But no. It's you."

"But you'd already met me?"

"Yes, but I'd met you as the shop girl, not as the artist. Why didn't you say you were the carver before?"

"Ottoh, you met him, he's insistent that some of the more traditional customers may balk at the idea of buying something like that made by a woman. Even if it's just a toy, people have come to know my father and his work."

"That sounds ridiculous."

"I think so too."

"Well, since your name isn't tied to the toy business, you can come to work for me."

"I can…" She looked up, shocked. "What?"

"Yes," his voice excitedly higher now. "That is why I wanted to talk to you and why I bought the sheep toy. I've spent the last two years rebuilding and refurbishing our main palace. I've brought in masons, painters, artisans of all kinds to make my home someplace worth being. But I have not found a sufficient carver or sculptor. But you. I saw the sculpting on the sheep, the detail, and I was curious. I saw the statue and knew I wanted something of that quality and artistry. Do you work quickly?"

"Well, that statue took me a bit, but I would say I do a decent job in a good amount of time."s

"Excellent. You're hired."

Peytra was stunned. A few moments ago, she'd been ready to smack this Duke, and now she'd been contracted to carve out his home. "How long will I take? And how much will it pay?"

"Oh, I'm not quite sure how long, but I would say there are two halls that need complete work, the frames and doors throughout as well. And if you're as skilled as I've seen, you may need to make a few free-standing pieces. I would say if you are like the mason, perhaps two to three years. And as for payment, I'll pay you salary. Twenty-five gold a season."

That could be about three hundred gold in the end, more than she had ever seen in her life. But she'd have to live around the Duke and away from home. "Thirty-Five gold a season."

"Twenty-seven."

"Thirty-four."

"Twenty-eight."

"Thirty and an entire set of custom tools."

"Deal." And they shook hands like old friends, but with the Duke's still encased in leather. Peytra was smiling, having received her first real work as a solitary artist. She looked at their hands and noted curiously that his hand was much larger than originally thought, but it held her hand with a deliberate sort of care. There was a knock at the workshop door, and they froze, hands still clasped.

"Your Grace. I have some drink." The page barged in and stopped like a stunned deer. "Excuse me, Your Grace. I did not know you had company." The page took a deep bow while the Duke and Peytra took their hands back, the latter running quickly out of her workshop. Her cheeks burned the entire way to the house, and she was glad when the cool rain touched at her face to quell the flush. Her heart rose up after having fallen from the contest. It beat rapidly in her breast.

Later in the night, the Duke ate and prepared for bed. Before lying on the work table, he gingerly placed the little sheep on the table next to where he slept.

CHAPTER 3

The carriage van glided smoothly on newly repaired wheels. Peytra felt the spring breeze through her loosened hair. She was sitting on a wagon following the carriage, watching as the farm homes and little towns sped by. The soldier sitting next to her leaned in. "Are you ok?" Peytra just smiled back. She was tired, but she was also undeniably excited.

Peytra ran through the events of the last night in her head, while the sun was high in the breezy afternoon. Her mother and father had been stunned with her sudden decision to leave and start her own career. Both her parents tried to convince her otherwise, but the money would help provide for the family altogether. Mikayel cautioned his daughter against the idea, as it was improper for a young woman to do something like that. But it was her mother that let it go, knowing that Peytra's art would make her happiest. Gerta spent the rest of the evening helping her daughter pack her valuables and tools to take along. All the while, she tried to dispense as much advice as she could. Her father, sadly, only repeated to watch out for any unruly guards or castle workers. And especially the Duke, he mentioned cryptically, as if he knew something he didn't trust.

As a sign of good faith, the Duke had bought the Fregh statue outright to display in his personal temple. It was traveling along with the Duke inside his carriage, still wrapped in that second-place velvet.

In the meantime, Peytra had disregarded her parent's caution and had begun to befriend a few of the guards. The one next to her, Georgie, seemed the most accepting of the situation. He had the tanned complexion and a face used to smiling. Georgie was from the Southern Island of Kauhle, to be exact, and he told her as much. They talked of his life there, in the mountainous tropics, before the conquest of a neighboring kingdom had caused his family to flee to this cold climate.

"And you? Where are you from?" he asked with glee.

Another guard, Hue, walked along next to the carriage. Hue was the guard who'd watched Peytra in the shop with such a keenly defensive eye. He'd been apprehensive of Peytra joining the troupe as a security precaution, but had warmed up to her in the process. Now the two old friends went on and on about their travels and adventures as formal soldiers before joining the Duke's guard. Hue would start the story, and Georgie would jump in with the details. Most of the conversation centered on different soldiering mishaps. Like the time that Hue picked a campsite much too close to a large colony of fire ants. Or the time Georgie was busy admiring his newly purchased dagger that he forgot to tie their traveling raft and all their other belongings were sent downstream. It was clear these two had gotten themselves in all sorts of trouble in their youth but had settled into more mature roles as they'd gone on.

Georgie attributed their lack of current adventures to Hue's (often floundering) courtship of Miss Biotie, the Duke's accountant. Georgie spent most of the trip giving Hue unwanted love advice. In answer, Hue would fiddle with the long, center-cut of his hair, or rub the shaved sides of his head with gloved fingers. Sometimes he'd offer a sudden loud chuckle at an idea.

Their banter entertained Peytra until they reached the Duke's castle late in the afternoon. The estate itself was surrounded by a thick and uncompromising wood. Many of the trees closest to the castle walls were saplings, which let Peytra know that all the foliage cover was deliberate. The walls surrounding the structure were close to thirty feet tall, and this was bordered in turn by a moat that must have been fifteen feet across. There were sections of the wall that were clearly newer than the rest. The shining, bleached stone a contrast to neighboring deep grey weathered walls, as if the castle had been sieged since its original construction.

"Does the Duke have any enemies?" Peytra asked Hue and Georgie.

Hue coughed uncomfortably. "What, what makes you say that?"

"Well, I mean, there's a lot of new growth, and the walls look like they've been rebuilt pretty recently. It's a fair guess that this castle has been attacked in the last few years."

"Oh, that." Georgie gave a big smile. "That was nothing, just a little skirmish due to his father. Nothing to worry about. Nothing at all."

"And you'll notice that His Grace has been very, um, cautious and really fortified his home. It's really just a precaution. Nothing out of the ordinary for these lord types," Hue interjected. "There's nothing to worry about here. The Duke is just a private person."

Peytra could clearly tell they were hiding something. There was some sort of threat that they most certainly didn't want her to know about. She wondered but was afraid to ask, if that skirmish the years before had been the cause of the damage to the Duke. Damage such that he was now compelled to hide every inch of skin beneath cloth, leather, and wood.

The drawbridge opened up, and the traveling party crossed the threshold into the main courtyard. Peytra almost lost her breath and fell off the wagon. Those tall, foreboding walls concealed something akin to a small city. Inside the outer walls were farm animals, crowds of workers, and well over a hundred guards all working around an extravagantly faced palace. The facade alone was an intricate, classic masterpiece. Peytra spotted the Duke's sigil aligning the archways. There was so much there – stained glass, filigree – that Peytra didn't quite know where to look.

"Yeah, I've forgotten the kind of sight the castle can be to newcomers," Hue said with a smile.

"It's a lot to take in," Peytra said.

"Well, I'll say this for our lord, it's a pretty nice place to live," said Georgie. "Speaking of His Grace, we have to escort him to his quarters. You better head over to the back area, and I'm sure someone'll get you to your proper rooms and such. Ask for Gani."

Georgie pointed to her destination, and Peytra jumped off the carriage as it slowed and waited at the end of the building. She stood with her satchel, absorbing the scene, and managed to see the Duke's oddly formal procession. For a few minutes, the activity in the courtyard stopped and focused on the guard who surrounded the carriage as it parked in front of the entrance. The doors to the elaborate building flung open as servants, Peytra assumed, stepped out and lined the outer pathway. The guards did similarly, each organized as if they'd rehearsed it thousands of times. Georgie stood by the carriage door and opened it, bowing to the Duke as he did so. The Duke stepped out, and to Peytra's surprise, even in his property he retained his coverings from head to toe. As he walked, each servant bowed in turn. For a moment, his head turned and he paused, looking in Peytra's direction. Even though they were hundreds of feet apart, she could see the blue of his eyes locking a steady gaze with hers. He turned around and perhaps said something to Hue, who bowed and went into the carriage. Hue took out Peytra's Fregh statue and carried it behind the Duke as they disappeared into the castle.

"Really? Get out of here! Really? He just hired you right then and there? Wow. Never seen His Grace be so impulsive," Korrinne said as she hacked away at some carrots. She had been the first of the castle to greet Peytra near the servant's entrance, and before she knew, Peytra was sitting in the kitchen retelling how'd she gotten to the castle.

Korrinne was short and boisterous with slightly curly brown-orange hair. She had a young face with deep inset smile lines and was quick with an enthusiastic exclamation. She also had a voice that carried and pitched throughout the stone walls. Peytra just sat in the kitchen eating away at the large courtesy dish of meats, breads, and cheeses Korrinne, or Kori as she insisted she be called, had placed in front of her.

"Well, I mean, when I'd met His Grace earlier, he'd been rather cryptic, but I guess he'd liked my work enough he didn't care about formality and that nonsense." Peytra took a bite out of the sweetened bread in front of her. "He's a bit strange, I give it." She noted with a sudden shock that she was already so comfortable around the kitchen hand.

"All nobles are strange in their own way, I think. There have been some that have visited the estate, and some are better than others. Lords and ladies can get mighty uptight if everything isn't done just so, but the higher up they are, the worse they get. At least His Grace isn't too demanding. But they aren't like you and me, they have all these other worries and quirks bred into them."

"I wouldn't say he isn't demanding," a girl walking in interjected. "He's asked me to make a small welcome cake by this evening for the new hired sculptor, which I'm going to guess is you. I'm Gani." The girl held out her hand. She was short with reddish-blonde curls framing a face that seemed too young to run a kitchen, but with the smirk of someone quite older.

"Peytra." She took Gani's hand and shook. "You're the head cook?"

"Head cook, head pain in the arse," Kori interjected under her breath but with a playful smile.

Gani replied with a smirk. "I said I wanted those carrots cubed, not sliced," she said dryly, "You'll have to start all over."

"Oh, come on! What's the difference?" Kori exclaimed.

"Cooking time in the stew. Anyway, don't throw

them out, I can use the sliced ones in tomorrow's dish."

Kori huffed around the kitchen, preparing to fix her mistake. Despite this, by their easy manner, it was clear that the two were close friends and thick as thieves.

"How'd you know I was the new hire?"

"Well, he said he'd hired a new sculptor, young and talented. Also, your bag and things are all over my kitchen. And finally, I could hear you from down the hall," Gani said, then tilted her chin up and raised her voice. "Someone," her eyes shifted, "is so loud!"

Kori just made a face and stuck out her tongue at Gani; both Gani and Peytra giggled. Thick as thieves indeed.

"Back to business," Gani continued, "what kind of cake do you like?"

※

Peytra was all too relieved to lay down in her new bed and new room. She'd just come from the servant's dinner where Gani had presented her with the promised cake. After their earlier conversation, which included Gani listing off at least twelve kinds of creams and their differences, they'd decided on a simple, fruited and cream cake. What made Peytra an immediate hit amongst the others was that she insisted on sharing, and Gani, predicting this, had made enough for everyone.

As her head rested on the pillow in her small private servant room, Peytra ran through the events of the day in her mind. She was miles from home now, in what was to be her new residence for the next few years. She'd met so many people she could barely remember all their faces, names, and positions. Her last encounter had been with Miss Biotie, the one for whom Hue pined for and the Duke's accountant. She was a tall, handsome woman with a thick accent from the Northeastern region. Even though Peytra only had a few moments to meet the woman, Miss Biotie, or Una as she asked to be called, gave off an aura of capability. This, despite the fact that Una spit her water in shock when Peytra informed her of how much the Duke had agreed to pay her. It wasn't that she didn't deserve that much, Una clarified, she was just shocked that he had agree to pay that much without consulting her.

"Well then," she went back to her cake, "I'll put that in the books. But that is quite strange. I hope I'm not out of a job soon." She smiled warmly and Peytra. She liked Una.

In fact, she liked them all. She tried to place their faces in her mind, and thought about the way she would carve them. *Pine and maple for Gani and Kori*, she thought, to show off their bright features. She'd carve them together, intertwined and whispering to one another, as they were at dinner. Georgie's features would do well in a dynamic hardwood, something like cypress. Peytra determined that Hue and Una would be especially interesting in a redwood. She delighted in the idea of carving their sharp features and how those features would shift and move in different lights.

Peytra stretched her arms above her and assessed her hands. Her fingers were short but deft. The padding on her palms and fingertips had long since calloused. These were strong hands, carver's and sculptor's hands that had shaped, made, and brought to life the images of her mind. Looking up, she thought about how she would shape the faces that had come into her life. How she'd move her thumb to sculpt the angle of a nose or eye. A thought crossed her mind: how would she carve a person like the Duke?

When Peytra had been a little girl, her father taught her about every wood type with different stories. There was a tree he used to love telling her about that was extinct now. The Sleeping Blackbark, which was known not just for its deep grey color, but for the way the sap of the tree could be used to make a clear lacquer. It was an old legend among woodworkers, and somehow its mystery seemed to evoke the Duke. But it would be difficult to ever carve the Duke without seeing his face. Yet, she knew she would like to paint that particular shade of blue of his eyes. Eyes that seemed to lock her in place in the stolen moments when they looked at her.

The other thing that Peytra had taken away from her chaotic day was that the Duke was good, but strange. Strange seemed fine to Peytra so long as it didn't interfere in her work or life. But there seemed to be a number of mysteries that continued to bother her while she should be sleeping. When had the castle been attacked? Were they still in danger? What had happened to the Duke to make him continue covering every inch of skin? Had he been mutilated by whoever had attacked the castle?

And then there was something else, the way he talked about Fregh like he knew the goddess, like she was more than just a pious story. This bothered Peytra in a way she couldn't quite recognize.

She stood up for a moment and went to her new mirror. In front was the washing pitcher, and she splashed herself with a bit of water to get a moment of clarity. She looked at herself in the candlelight. Her large, almond eyes looked more tired than they felt. Just a day ago, she'd been a young woman pacing home dejected from a festival contest. She'd been living as a craftsperson in the shadow of the name of her father. But here she was now, about to begin her journey as an artist for this mysterious Duke. Alone, and in a strange castle. Peytra didn't know why, but she was afraid for what was to come. Something beyond excitement or professional fear was building at the pit of her stomach, and she couldn't name it. But she would have to accept that it was there for now.

CHAPTER 4

"My goodness." Kori looked over at Peytra at breakfast. "You look horrible."

Peytra could almost feel the kick that Gani gave Kori under the table.

"What she means to say is that you don't look like you got a lot of sleep," said Gani.

"No, no, I didn't. This is a bit of a change for me. Also, someone kept pacing above my room, and it kept waking me up," answered Peytra. That was true, aside from her nerves, Peytra kept waking up to the seemingly random steps from above. Each dream or nightmare abruptly ended with the pounding of boots above. With huge bags beneath her eyes and an overall disheveled appearance, it was clear her nerves had done a toll on her

"Oh that! Must have been the changing or shifting of the guard. It can be a bit jarring if you never stayed at a place like this before," Kori said.

"I don't think so. I could sometimes hear the guard change. It was different. This pacing or stomping – it stopped and started a lot. I don't know. Maybe it's being in new walls that is doing it after all," Peytra said, taking a fresh piece of toast.

Una sat down near the trio with a plate of bread and fruit. "Oh my. You look horrible!" she exclaimed, looking up at Peytra. "Are you sick?"

Gani just smacked herself in the forehead.

"New place jitters," Kori answered for Peytra.

"Oh, well, are you feeling up to today? You're the Duke's first scheduled meeting. I can move it if you need to get some rest," Una said, not noticing Kori stealing a few fresh grapes off her plate.

"No, no. It's fine. I'm excited to get to work," Peytra said. She just wanted everyone to leave her appearance alone and was growing ever frustrated at something so trivial.

"Well then, I'm going to need a list of supplies. Also, you'll be meeting the Duke in the hour."

Peytra swallowed a small bite in answer.

<hr />

Una made it clear on the walk over that if Peytra ever got lost on her way to meet the Duke, she was to ask for the meeting room. Not his office, library, or personal study. That last room was off-limits to most members of the household and forbidden to all guests. Una didn't even know where in the castle the study was, only a faint awareness of the room's location. Peytra considered that as just one more way in which the Duke was strange.

The meeting room itself was sparsely furnished but painfully elaborate at the same time. In the center was a large oak table with filigree carving on the sides. Peytra looked at it and noted its quality. She remembered something faint in the back of her mind, a memory of her father doodling in a notebook and telling her that the mark of many old masters was how well they could render two things:

myrtle and linden flowers. Peytra looked at the filigree a bit closer and saw that patterned among it were clusters of myrtle. This table must have been at least a hundred years old. At the same time, that little memory of her father teaching her the history of their trade opened a little knotted feeling in her throat. But she took a moment to push the sudden homesickness away.

Along one wall was a short bookcase, also exquisitely carved. Along the walls were various portraits in gold frames and a few tapestries. Despite all of the decoration, the room was large enough to not feel cluttered. But it also had the unwanted effect of making the meeting feel very cold and impersonal.

After some bowing and some formalities, they sat around the table. The Duke was seated singularly at one side. There were guards and attendants posted at the four corners of the room, as immobile as statues. Peytra tried to see if she recognized any of them, but no, these were all new people. She tried to look one in the eye, but they stood perfectly, frighteningly still.

Due to the setting and the stillness of the guards, Peytra thought that this would be a painfully boring and formal meeting. As she sat down, however, the Duke's masked face looked over to her and exclaimed, "Peytra, You look horrible! Have you taken ill already here? I can request that my physician see you." He began to wave to an attendant, but Peytra had taken enough already this early in the morning.

"For the good goddesses' ever-living sake!" she said, mentally smashing the carving of him in her mind. "I'm fine! Let's just get this over with." For a moment, the room held its breath. The page stood in his tracks. Peytra had raised her voice to the Duke. Never having grown up around the nobility, she was not trained in the business of monitoring oneself in the presence of the higher-born. But even now, by the complete, uncomfortable silence, she was keenly aware that she had committed a dear mistake. She looked over at him, speechless and unable to read his expression behind the mask he still wore.

After a moment, his tone strained to sound matter-of-fact. "Well then," he cleared his throat uncomfortably, "let us get to it." Peytra could almost swear she detected a wounded tone in the Duke's voice.

The meeting went by as smoothly as it could after the fact, albeit Peytra still felt as if she was balanced on the edge of a cliff. It seemed the Duke wanted to move on from her little faux pas. They discussed supplies and what she would have to do. One of the pages and Una were to take her to the doors and doorways she would be carving first after the meeting.

"And what would Your Grace like carved on the doorways and such? Your sigil? A set of patterns or something more involved?" Peytra asked, now trying to imitate Una's professional speech pattern.

"Hmm, well. There are seven doors, are you familiar with the 'Trials of the Polodians?'"

"Is that the story about one of the first children of Fregh who angered the sky gods and all that?"

"Yes," the timbre of his voice showed that that boyish excitement had come back to the Duke.

"I think I remember the stories, Your Grace. My mother used to tell me the tales when I was little, but it's been long."

"Ah. Well." He dramatically cleared his throat. "There were five Polodians, and you can carve a door for each one's trial, one doorway for the curse and a final one for when they are reunited."

"I think I remember some of the stories. One swam through the ocean in a giant shell, I think. Another had a trial by fire, if I'm correct. The one that disguised himself as a tree and had the forest help him escape was my favorite."

"Ellith, yes, yes, that's my favorite as well. I thought the way he tricked away from his captors was ingenious," added the Duke, obviously enjoying the exchange.

Peytra smiled, recalling the way her mother would pull the blanket over herself to imitate Ellith's disguise. The pang of homesickness was nursed by the warmth of the memory. "I think that story is why I like red carving oak so much."

Una interjected at this point, looking at a clock on the far wall. "We have several histographies in the castle, should you wish to read them on your own. Or Marcus, the librarian could help you."

"Should be interesting. I'll need to take measurements and make a few drafts before I begin carving."

"That should be fine," said the Duke his voice subtly shifted to a colder tone. Peytra wasn't sure, but he seemed dejected at not being able to tell her the stories himself.

They finished their meeting and were dismissed. The page and Una escorted Peytra to the doorways she would be working on. Peytra was shocked at the size of the doors and doorways but was determined not to show it. If anything, she didn't want to seem any less professional than she already felt she had. However, the doorways themselves were well over a man and a half's height at their shortest ends, and much larger than she had ever worked with. Each was a deeply grained dark wood.

"What is this?" Peytra asked while petting the grain.

"Ah, it's mahogany. The Duke had it imported." Una looked into her notebook, seemingly distracted. "Did the Duke seem, well, strange to you today?"

"Hmm? What do you mean? He's been that odd since I met him." Peytra couldn't take her eyes off the rich undertones of the wood.

"Yes, you know, that, he's quite, well," Una looked up at the archway, "I just wonder whether he is ill. Or worse, struck by the madness."

"What? Madness? Well, since I've met him, he's been that way. I thought all nobles were that changeable and excitable. You know, like us folk can be."

Una dropped her voice and made a furtive glance. "Well, yes, I'm sure they can be, but this Duke, as long as any of us have known him, has always been a touch more measured. Never raising his voice or showing much more than quiet regard. But Hue has mentioned that something is up with His Grace. On his trip, he made impulsive decisions and seemed suspect to moodiness. And here this morning, he began to get so excitable. And, no offense to you, but never once has he hired anyone, for any project, without consulting me or the accounts. It's quite alarming if you…." Her lips closed abruptly as a page walked through the room. "You know, ask Kori later tonight," she added one more time before the case was closed.

Peytra's day went by quickly as she set herself to begin the massive project. Despite her lack of sleep the previous night, the work energized her. Yet something haunted the back of her mind. The Duke's temperament was something that concerned the others employed in the household. As a child, she'd heard tales of the ways in which her people lived and died on the whims of their rulers. But Kings, Dukes, Counts, and such always seemed so far away from their little home. She did remember something about the former Duke being a tyrant when she was a just a babe, which was a reason why her family retreated to the country rather than live in their city. But her parents rarely spoke about it in front of her and the siblings. Thus far, the Duke had struck her as emotional and eccentric from his interests and the quick changes to his voice. But it was hard to conceive of what type of man he might be behind that mask.

CHAPTER 5

It was late after the servants' dinners, and after the Duke and some of the officers had retired to their quarters, that some of the employees sat around the large kitchen fire. Una was fixing figures in her ledger; Hue sat to the other corner so he could regularly gaze up at her, her angled features dancing in the candlelight. Hue was shining a section of old armor that had rusted almost through. Georgie stuffed an impossibly elaborate pipe with good tobacco and smoked it leisurely on a stool. Gani was at the counter, re-bottling her spices and cursing the poorly written labels under her breath. Then there was Peytra. She had decided that, like the others, she wished to look a little productive if possible. She'd brought a small slab of wood to keep her busy, and thus she whittled at it absentmindedly, seated on the floor with her legs crossed, shavings spilling into the bowl of her skirt..

There were a few strangers to Peytra, seated here and there in the kitchen with them. Another member of the guard, a page, a few maids. Each of them doing their own little handicrafts. It remained unsaid that the atmosphere was deliciously secretive. It was one of friends holding in their gossip, eager to relate the most contraband of news to one another.

Una had done the honor of asking Kori to give a history of the Duke quietly during dinner. She entered now, carrying some old knitting and sat on the chair closest to the fire, a clear place of honor. Kori seemed older in the orange glow of it. Gani looked over with a smirk; she seemed familiar with the way Kori would begin a story. She cleared her voice dramatically and began:

"This, friends, this tain't a story about our Gracious Duke, who treats us kindly and pays us well. No, this is the story of his father, the fright-ning Red Duke, His Grace Willem Ameros IV. So, as I say these things, friends, let's be clear that these words done never left my lips, or else you be the one welcome to leave," she said with a long pause to look around. No one so much as shifted in their seat let alone left.

She stuck her needles back into her yarn and continued. "Long-go, before I was born, my Ma and Pa worked this very castle when His Grace Willem was young and handsome. He stood a head taller than all the men, with a great mane of golden hair. He was fit, with a jaw that were as stern and chiseled as the rock face of this very castle. Least to say, this man were a beautiful one, who smiled and joked and were lively. In those days, before he became the Red Duke, the dashing Willem was charming. He had lady suitors from all over this land and all other lands traveling to our humble home to see him and try to convince him to court them. He may have courted many for fun, but none, not even the richest Queen from the Blue Eve Isles, could conquer his heart.

"'Cept one day came the mysterious woman with the flaming hair. The Lady had eyes of the clearest blue, skin with not one scar or blemish. But twas her hair that you could see in the distance, a bright but deep crimson that, when hit by sunlight, looked as if she were aflame. She were the most beautiful creature that may have walked the earth. Even more beautiful than His Grace Willem himself. And she appeared one afternoon, with no title, no caravan, and no name at the door of the palace. My Pa remembered it, how she walked in, asking to be escorted to see the famous handsome Duke. Well, none cared that this woman had no title, for she had looks to rival the gods themselves! The page did as she commanded, and the Duke Willem, he who had been courted by all the most agreeable and accomplished and richest women in the world, and not conquered by one, looked at this mysterious woman and fell instantly in love.

"They were wed soon after, and soon after that she bore Willem a son, our Duke Jors Ameros. She refused to give her name, so instead, they called her Lady Swan, for she had the grace of a swan swimming across the water. The Lady was loved by the servants of the Duke. She was kind and gracious. The Lady Swan loved all things that were of beauty. She thrived on music and the arts, and good foods. But what she loved most dearly was her young son, who would grow to be our beloved Duke Jors. As Jors grew into a young boy, he was doted on by the Mistress. But as the years went on, the Duke Willem grew a bit older and greyer. He were still handsome, no doubt, but the Lady Grey seemed ageless. He also grew colder. He would snap at the servants and guards. He no longer seemed to care about the Dukedom. Yet, all seemed fine as they could be in those times.

"Then, one evening, I remember well. There

were a fearsome storm. The wind itself blew the tops off the stables. It raged, and the rain pounded against the windows like they were to break. My pa remembered that night clear as day up until he passed. He was mopping up some of the incoming waters at the door when a cloaked figure ran past him out of the house. He could see her red hair and knew twas the Lady Swan.

"'Mistress! Mistress! Don't go out there!' he called. He tried to run after her, but she were a woman possessed. She ran so fast out into the courtyard, she almost looked like she were flying. The guards, my pa, and the Duke Willem himself ran after her, but before they could catch her...."

"CRASH!" Kori clapped her hands loudly, and all were taken aback. "Lightning struck the ground where she stood. They searched for her body all day and night, but twas like she'd disappeared. Burned up total by that lightning. Not even a pile of ash left in her place." Kori took an unspoken moment of silence to mourn the loss of the Lady Swan, and the rest of the room followed.

She looked up and continued: "Maybe twas heartbreak, or maybe he'd been growing steadily cruel and we'd ignored it in the light of Lady Swan. After that, the Duke twas more fearsome than we'd ever seen and grew worse as the years went on. He would beat the servants for the smallest thing. He was petty to his subjects and put forth ridiculous laws on a whim. He insisted on whipping those who broke his laws himself. That's when he earned the name of Red Duke, for he joked that his favorite color was red, not for the color of his late mistresses' tresses, but for the wounded skin of his subjects.

"Though in all this, none experienced more ire from the Red Duke than his son Jors. Perhaps he was as hated by his father as he had been loved and doted on by his late mother. He was growing into a handsome young man. Kind, smart, athletic, with a beautiful countenance and the blue eyes of his mother. But unlike his father, he was even-tempered. But the Duke would beat him just the same, cuff his ears in front of the visitors or humiliate him when possible. Jors, now our good Duke, was silent 'til the day the attack came.

"Now, I'll be honest, I dun remember much of the day, everything were too loud and painful and chaotic. But about seven years ago, as the fall were turning to winter, an army appeared. They stood out there, frightening like a-lined headstones into the distance. The envoy came towards the gates and demanded to speak with the famed Duke. Duke Willem came forth in anger and demanded to know why an army had dared trespass on his lands. The envoy said they would leave peacefully on just one condition: They demanded the body of Jors Amero. The Duke Willem, not caring for his son and perhaps resenting those blue eyes he shared with his mother, did the unspeakable and the mad. He said yes.

"All the guards refused to escort the young Jors to what was surely death. So Duke Willem dragged his son out by his hair. He screamed and begged and cried. But the Duke's hatred of his son persisted, and perhaps, we all thought, he'd finally gone mad. The envoy had Jors put in a cage, shackled like some animal. Then, the adolescent Jors, with the soft voice and golden hair, let out a scream that stopped us all. Twas then that like a spell came over all of us. All the servants felt the sudden, painful need to save our future Duke and the heir to these lands. We were grabbed by the fervor and need to protect him. We marched out of kitchens. We marched out of the stables. We came in out of the fields. We was grabbing whatever was handy and started to fight. Even the Duke, perhaps finally overcome by fatherly duty, pulled out his whip and sword to the invading army. It was grisly and bloody, but none would stop, nor could stop until Jors was safe. The guards ran forth, hurling and clashing their weapons against the enemy. The maids chucked candlesticks and silverware. The cooks poured boiling oil from the castle walls. Stones went flying, and as if it were all slowed down, bodies along both lines began to tumble. The damage has given the castle so many scars. So many of us died that day. Even my…"

Kori fiddled with her knitting needles. Gani came over and put one hand on the storyteller's shoulder to give it a warm, intimate squeeze. She took a breath and continued, "In the end, the Duke was horribly wounded, and the invading army conceded. But as they walked the young Jors back to the castle, an arrow lit with a green fire flew through the sky. Was like an arrow shot by Protratrium, the god of death himself. It hit Jors square in the back, but did not kill him. Instead, it lit him aflame, and he seemed consumed by it. He let out the most tear-curdling cry anyone would hear then or forever.

"They put out the fire on the young Jors and covered him with a blanket. That were the last time anyone ever saw his face. He holed himself up in his room for weeks. His father, Duke Willem, died a slow, agonizing death from the wound he'd gotten. It became green and septic, he grew feverish and repentant. In the end, he died alone, attended to by a few maids that didn't hate him as much as they should have. He paid for his cruelty, for even his son, though he called for him, refused to show him his face.

"Then our Jors became Duke, and while he may

MASK OF THE NOBLEMAN

be too burned to show his face, he's been a good and fair Duke. He shows much the grace of Lady Swan without the anger of Duke Willem. Maybe one day, he won't feel the need to hide his face, however burned or misshapen, to the loyal servants that we are. And we all pray he stay that same good Duke, with an even temper, no matter how hidden he may be. But it's getting late, and we all have work in the morning. Night, lovelies," and with that, Kori gathered up her needles and headed to her quarters. All of them cleared away, comforted by the story.

Peytra looked down at her little woodwork, and she realized she had absentmindedly carved the beginnings of a bear.

CHAPTER 6

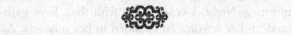

Peytra found little satisfaction in the drafts she'd created until she finally visited Marcus. It'd been years since she'd heard the stories of the Polodians, and her memory was clouded by all the stories she'd heard since then. What surprised Peytra about Marcus was how young he was. She pictured an elderly, bent over figure would be the Duke's librarian. Instead, it was a tall, good-looking young man just a few years older than herself. He had a mop of chestnut hair, clean-shaven face, and roguish eyes. He was the type of man her sister Marii would refer to as "trouble". He didn't even seem to see the need to wear scholar's robes, just pants and a light white shirt that was just open enough to show the beginnings of a well-defined chest. No, this was a man that most like bedded the maids of the castle regularly.

Peytra was not surprised then when his first look to her was one of a predator suddenly seeing new prey. She would refuse to be the rabbit in his wolf-like trap.

"Well, I see that the newest resident has deigned to grace me with her presence," Marcus said, bowing, "It is my pleasure to be at your service. Or did you come just to admire the view?"

"How did you know I was new?"

"For one, you look like you have never seen a place such as this in your life. For another, I know almost every resident. Many, rather intimately."

He was baiting her, but she had seen enough men like that. The type of salesmen with no goods to sell. Her best bet was to ignore his advances outright. "I'm here, because I'm told you can give me some information on the Polodians for the lintels I am here to carve. If you're done, I would appreciate a book on the subject."

"My dear! Why read a dry text when I can recite it from memory? Then you won't be able to resist my charms." He smiled rougishly and wiggled his eyebrows. Peytra suppressed a smile.

She thought she could be immune to his charms, but perhaps didn't realize how easy it was to be swept up in the moment by him.. As he recited the histography to her, he was bombastic and grand. For a few moments, she was spellbound by the movements of his hands across the page, the inflection in his rich voice and the shape of him. To combat this, she was a touch colder than usual. She could not let herself end up troubled by this man before she'd finished this commission.

Being around Marcus did inspire something in her. Peytra channeled that into her drafts. Now that she knew more of the stories, they seemed to draw themselves in front of her. The ideas spilled out of her and onto the chalk.

At the next meeting with the Duke where she presented her drawings, he was, for her, suspiciously silent as he looked through. He shuffled one through the other, and it all made her distinctly uncomfortable.

"You'll notice, Your Grace, that I've created two separate patterns to differentiate the water and the wind in Metonia's relief. That way, it will look like the clamshell she rides to cross the ocean will look as if it is pushed and pulled by the two," she said. He only nodded. "And, Your Grace, you see the angle I've made Reduux and his mountain? That way, as the light changes from the high windows in that room throughout the day, the shadows on the carving will make him look like he is climbing as the sun sets."

Again he nodded. Peytra was getting nervous, fearing that he did not like them, that he'd taken her to be a charlatan. She feared she would be fired outright and sent packing home. As she was already trying to come up with explanations to give to her parents for her return, the Duke let out a chuckle. "Umm, Your Grace?"

"Oh, nothing, just – I remember something funny about Juliana's story, of how she dressed in sheepskin to escape her captors. My nurse, when I was a child, always pronounced 'sheep' wrong. Just something I haven't thought in about in a very long time."

"Ah." Peytra smiled. Maybe he did like the drafts.

"Hmm, this portrait of Robino strongly resembles Marcus."

"Oh, well, I had just recently seen him when I was fixing these, and I suppose it just…"

"The drafts are approved," the Duke said with an odd force to his voice. "You may begin immediately, just change Robino's face a bit. We'd not like Marcus to get more of an ego than he already has."

The downpour came a few days after Peytra began the relief carving. It was the type of rain that slowed everything down. No one seemed to want to work, but rather retreat close to the fire. Even Peytra, who could usually throw herself into her craft, found herself slowed by the weather. At the same time, she felt irritated and restless. There wasn't just rain, but thunder and lightning. Every time she heard the thunder, she imagined the Lady Swan running into a field only to be struck by it.

Dinner was quiet, and many retired early. Peytra spent hours trying to sleep, but something seemed to irk her. Then she heard it, the pounding above her on the wooden ceiling. It was loud and uneven. She knew it wasn't the guards because she'd memorized the guard patterns. It irked her such that, instead of sleeping, she decided she may as well alleviate her curiosity. She lit a candle, dressed, and left her room to explore.

In the dark, as the shadows made the stone walls dance, she felt her way to the servants' stairs. They curved around to the back end of the castle. Peytra had never been here; before her was a long, thin stone and wood-faced hallway. She was acutely aware of the thunder and rain pounding outside. There were floor-to-ceiling tapestries every few feet, but it was too dark to see their design. She searched for the area that would be right above her room. She didn't see a door, just another tapestry. Then, at her feet, she felt warm air coming from the floor. She felt behind the tapestry, finding a door. Peytra took a leap of faith by blowing out her candle to step behind.

She opened the door. Before she could stop herself, she realized the sort of mistake she may be making. What if she was intruding on a private moment? What if the noise she had heard was someone like Marcus seducing someone? It was too late. Peytra found herself in a small cluttered space with a large, roaring fire. There was a grand seat with its back to her. Above the large cushioned back, she could see tufts of reddish-blonde curls.

"Stop. Who goes there?" the voice from the chair said. For a moment, Peytra didn't recognize it. Then she realized she'd heard it before. It was the Duke's voice but unmuffled by the mask. Oh, she would be fired for sure! Perhaps jailed or whipped for intruding on the Duke uninvited.

"I said, who goes there? Answer!"

She'd never heard him raise his voice like this. She gasped. "Forgive me, Your Grace. Please, please, please. I just – I was trying to find the source of the noise. I did not mean to intrude, please. Please do not fire me. Please. I'm so sorry."

"Peytra," he breathed. "It's fine, just please, turn around and close your eyes." Peytra did as she was told and then began to fear some worse punishment was to be bestowed on her. "Yes, Your Grace." She was getting ready to cry as she stood there in self-imposed darkness.

"You may turn around now."

Peytra opened her eyes and saw that the Duke was now in his regular complete covering. His mask was on, and he was adjusting his gloves. "I'm so sorry. Your Grace, please, forgive me, I did not..."

He raised a hand to quiet her. "It's fine. Why did you come here?"

"Well, Your Grace, I wasn't looking for you, I was looking for the source of the noise."

"Noise?"

"Yes, Your Grace. My room is below this one, and sometimes I hear loud steps and I couldn't sleep because of the storm, and well, I wanted to know who or what was causing the noise."

"I come here when I can't sleep. It's one of the few places I have complete privacy."

"Again, my apologies, Your Grace."

"We can have your room moved if you'd like."

"That won't be necessary, Your Grace. Now that I know what the noise is and my imagination isn't running away from me, I'll be able to sleep."

"Well, you are welcome to go, or, um," he cleared his throat, "if you'd like, you can join me. But I'd rather this not get out to the rest of the staff."

She thought for a moment. There was something deliciously wicked about the idea of sitting in a room alone with the strange Duke. To have a secret shared only with him seemed like a risk worth taking. Especially on a night such as this, with the storm and her thoughts keeping her awake. He was an odd one, though, wanting privacy then asking her to stay with him. Peytra decided it would be rude to refuse. She also knew that she would remain curious then entire night if she left.

"I can stay, Your Grace. I have too much trouble sleeping during the storm."

He nodded and waved her towards a couch that was close to the fireplace. He took his place in his oversized seat perpendicular to her. She took in her surroundings. The seats were plush but worn. The fireplace was built from simple brick, and above the mantel hung a portrait of a beautiful red-haired woman standing against a pillar holding a rose. Peytra realized that that must be the Lady Swan, his mother. She truly was beautiful, with symmetrical features that were both elegant and soft. Something about the portrait seemed oddly familiar to Peytra. As if she'd seen the face before but she couldn't quite place it. It was haunting some part of her memory.

"My mother," said the Duke, noticing her fascination with the portrait. "This used to be my father's private study."

"She was quite beautiful, Your Grace."

"Yes. Yes, she was. The portrait is good, but it doesn't quite capture her. I don't know that anything could."

"You know, she looks like Fregh, or what I think Fregh would look like, if she, you know... I mean, your mother even had the long red-hair that they say Fregh had."

He chuckled. "It's funny. I know everyone thinks it when they see this portrait, but no one ever says it. Everyone thought it when she was here as well, but no one seemed to have the gall to say it then either."

"Well, I mean, it's obvious though, isn't it? All the stories, they say something about the most beautiful woman with red hair. I mean, if I met a man with an eye-patch, a beard, and a peg-leg, I'd say they looked like Drindon."

He laughed at this. "You know, once I went to a smaller township in my protection on the other end of the coast. Every year they host a 'Drindon' look-alike contest. Well, all the old men put on eye-patches and fake wooden legs that day. They all lose their depth perception and can't walk on the legs; what you get is old men stumbling through the town. Doesn't help that all the bars make their beer free that day."

Peytra laughed. "I can imagine. I could also imagine my brothers trying to get my Da in on the action. Or they'd just enter themselves. I know Lukas would, he loves doing impressions."

"How many brothers do you have?"

"Well, I have three older brothers. Thom, Lukas, and Peytire – Peety we call him. The two oldest are married, so I have two sisters through them, Evete and Muriall. Then I have two older sisters, Helene and Marii. Helene married Mikael, so I have a brother through that."

"That's a large family."

"It is. But it's a good one."

"You mentioned before that you're the youngest. And that you don't look like your siblings."

"Yes. But my family never treated me different." Peytra was annoyed. She hated when people brought that up. He must have noticed the change in her voice and changed the subject.

"How does a girl end up a master carver?"

"Well, I'm not *really* a master. I'd have to apprentice with someone outside my father for that to be admitted in the guild. But when I was just a toddler, I would watch my father work. One day, I just picked up his tools and started working."

"And they took no issue to their daughter taking on something like that?"

"Well, I'm sure smaller minded people might have, but my parents were happy I wanted to learn a trade. They wanted all their children to learn some trade. And carving, sculpting was that skill I wanted to learn. I'm good at it," she paused, searching for an explanation, "but it's more than that. It draws me. I don't know what it is, exactly, but it's like the wood speaks to me. People, they see a tree limb or a block and they just see that limb or block. But I see something different. I look at the grooves and the lines, the imperfections, and I see the shape it wants to be. I see its potential to be something that makes people feel something when they see it. It's getting to be the same with clay and stone. With stone, you aren't chipping away to shape, you let it shape itself. You're revealing what it is at its core. Clay and plaster, that's a bit more difficult. Those materials are temperamental, and they don't say things the way wood and stone do, but in time you just have to work with each other. Let it settle in the ways it needs. I know this sounds mad, but that's how I feel when I work. That I'm just letting the materials be what they want to be. That they speak with and through me."

Peytra looked towards the Duke. He was enshrined in the large seat, enveloped in the darkness of his black clothing. Beneath the mask, the only signs of life were his clear blue eyes, locked in an intense gaze with her. He was still, having let her finish. Peytra was flustered for a moment. She wasn't sure if she'd just come off as mad to her employer or just odd. She desperately craved to see his face to better understand how he saw her.

"It's quite funny that you deny being a master when you remind me of some of the best masters I have ever met. Just the way you talk about it. In many ways, your speech reminds me a bit of Master Tochtem. He was the Master Craftsman here for many years until his death."

"I've heard of Tochtem. My father spoke highly of him."

"He was quite excitable, but I think that drove his genius. He's the one that did the facade of the castle."

"He did? It's so complex, and it's a lot to measure up to. He must have had a clear, deft hand by the sharpness of lines he used."

"That is true." He moved his gaze to the other

side of the room. "Would you like to see something else he made?"

"Yes! Yes, I would."

He got up and traveled to a large bureau and picked up something small, then walked it over to her and placed it in her hands. She looked down at it. It was a small, intricately carved wooden box. She traced the outline of a Swan and a Bear. Tochtem had made much of the filigree go along the grain, which made the designs look made by nature. Peytra was enchanted with the artistry and the craftsmanship. The figures were dynamic, the swan with its wings outspread, the bear, reared on its hind legs. But the subtle lines in the expression made them look less like they were to fight but to dance.

Peytra traced a finger along the line of the Swan.

"The Swan is for my mother, who they referred to as the Lady Swan. The Bear is my father's sigil. It's attached to the Ameros name."

"It's beautiful. The lines are so delicate and sharp. You can tell it's a master's woodwork."

"It is quite nice. Would you like to see something interesting?" She nodded in reply. He held out his gloved hand, and she gave him back the box. He pointed to the base and then pressed a small rose on the side. Out popped a hidden compartment. "I used to hide little bobbles in here as a child." He handed it back to Peytra. She opened and closed the little compartment. It was clear that she was fascinated with how well the little device was rendered.

"This is amazing! I've never seen anything so cleanly made and rendered! The inner mechanism works so smoothly. My father would love this."

"It's yours if you'd like."

"Your Grace! No. I couldn't. That is much too kind."

"It's fine. It's clear you get much more joy from it than I have in a long while. This castle is littered with Tochtem's work. It will be fine."

On the one hand, Peytra would love to own a piece such as this, as something to aspire to. On the other, she felt that to take a gift such as this would be gravely inappropriate. Yet, this entire encounter was odd and inappropriate.

"If it would assuage your guilt, I could command you to keep it, but I'd rather not."

"I'll accept it. Thank you, Your Grace."

"In here, if you'd like," he hesitated for a moment, measuring his words, "you may call me by my name. Jors."

"Well, thank you for this beautiful gift, Jors."

He breathed in. There was something about the way she said his name that stirred a deep affection in him. "You're very welcome, Peytra." He was adept at controlling his voice for emotion, but perhaps he'd let something slip, for Peytra felt something small flutter in her chest. It was involuntary and strange, but it warmed her.

They spoke for a few more minutes, but something in the air had changed. Peytra listened to her more reasonable voice and then dismissed herself to bed, leaving the Duke alone in his study. He sat back down in his solitary seat, nursing the memory of her presence. He removed his mask and gloves, then felt the face he could never show her.

Back in her room, Peytra placed the little box on her night table. She decided its secret compartment would be the best place to hide her roughly carved bear figurine. She pinned her braids up and lay in bed. With her head on the pillow, she looked up at the ceiling. Instinctively she could still feel him up there, sitting in his large chair. Once it would have produced some anxiety to be in such close proximity to such a strange, powerful individual. At this moment, she felt comforted by his presence so near. He was strange, but he was kind to her.

CHAPTER 7

The coming days found the castle in a flurry of activity. Una was inundated with shifting and new accounts. She was left to stay up at night, counting out the season's pay. Kori and Gani were beginning preparations for the Summer menu. Hue and Georgie were running drills for new recruits. Thus Peytra was left alone to throw herself into her work.

Well, mostly alone. Marcus had finished his orders and cataloguing the week previous and felt that his new hobby would be to pester the newest female resident. Peytra, for her part, was not eager to be seduced by this known playboy. She was curt, rude, and sarcastic to him, but that only seemed the embolden the archivist. There was a safety in their flirtation, at least Peytra felt so. It had come to her attention through Kori and Gani that Marcus regularly bedded women for sport. At the very least, he was honest with his intentions. Peytra respected that, but she was not searching for short-lived affection. To her, their banter was play. It was enjoyable but not serious.

. . .

Late in the afternoon, Peytra was chiseling the archway and lost in the piece when she heard from the base of her scaffolding, "And how is my little woodpecker today?"

"Busy," Peytra answered back to Marcus without bothering to turn around.

"Ah, I see. Much too busy to eat then? Hmm? You must be hungry, though. Gani said you hadn't been to the kitchen since breakfast. But look here, I have gallantly brought you some lunch like the gentleman than I am. The only caveat is that you'll have to join me down here, birdie."

"I'm not hungry," but Peytra could feel a pang in her stomach that she'd been ignoring while she was lost in the work.

"Oh, come now, birdie, you can't well chip away at that on an empty stomach? You need your strength to keep pecking away. Come down, lunch with me to regain your strength, and then you can get back to all that laboring."

Peytra decided that a quick lunch and then shooing him away would be best for them both. "Fine, but you're to leave me be after that."

"But of course! I swear it on the crown."

Peytra climbed down, and he had brought water, cheese, bread, and fruit, which they picked at. Marcus went on about the texts he was planning on acquiring or having copied. They discussed some of the happenings of the castle and such. Peytra was getting up to get back to work when Marcus turned to her. "Well, shouldn't I get a small token for my efforts?"

"I said, 'thank you,' didn't I?"

"Yes, but you didn't show thanks."

"I swear, Marcus, do not try me, or I'll find a way to murder you in your sleep."

"Oh, birdie, if you want to come to my room at night, there are much more entertaining things we can do instead." He raised an eyebrow and gave her a roguish smile.

This utter bastard, Peytra thought to herself, *he'd be easier to deal with if he wasn't so handsome.* "Just spit it out, Marcus. What do you want?"

"Oh, just a kiss."

"No."

"Oh, birdie, just a small one on the cheek. A kiss between friends really." He tapped a sculpted cheek.

"And then you'll leave me to work?"

"But of course! I'll be on my merry way, and you can get back to beautifying the castle more than you already too."

Peytra was curious to do this, but she was sure to make a show of contempt. "Fine."

She leaned forward to where he was seated on the scaffolding. Just as she had pursed her lips and was about to touch them to his cheek, she heard a loud cough that caused her to turn mid-kiss. This meant that the kiss she was to place on Marcus's cheek ended on his lips.

"Well, now! That's more than I even asked for, birdie!" Marcus said, with a large, victorious smile on his face. Then there was another deliberate cough, and both turned to face the source. It was the Duke.

"Your Grace," Marcus said calmly.

"Your Grace," Peytra said in a panic. She averted her eyes and stared at the floor.

"Afternoon, I was just coming by to check on your progress. It seems you're working along. Are you having any trouble?"

"No, Your Grace. I was just, umm, having lunch.

I'll get back to work." Peytra could feel her cheeks burn but wasn't sure why.

"Feel free to rest if you need be. Either way, Marcus, how fortuitous that I should run into you. We have to leave in the early light tomorrow for Relinki."

"Oh? Why so sudden, Your Grace?"

"I have to settle a land dispute between two minor nobles, and I could use your skills in contract drafting."

"Well, I will gladly be prepared to join, Your Grace."

"That is appreciated, Marcus." The Duke turned and headed to leave. "You are welcome to return to your work now if you wish."

"Your Grace," Peytra and Marcus said in unison as he walked out.

"Well, Birdie," Marcus turned to Peytra with a mischievous look on his face, "care to give me another kiss for the road?"

As an answer, Peytra threw his used napkin in his face and climbed back up the scaffolding. He read enough in her discontent to leave her then. She got back to work with a rigorous fury. But every so often, she touched her hand to her lips. This was not her first kiss. She'd kissed a number of boys as an adolescent, but this was different. Something about that moment seemed wrong. There was also an intonation in the Duke's voice that was painfully cold. For whatever reason, it hurt her in a way that seemed foreign and uncomfortable. She took to chipping the archway, using the confusion as the force behind her mallet.

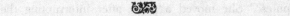

That night, unable to sleep, she heard a familiar sound. The Duke was stomping around his study, and this time the steps seemed louder than usual. Peytra wasn't sure if he was being deliberate until, a few moments later, she heard rhythmic knocking on her ceiling. She was sure he was trying to get her attention. Despite their earlier, awkward interaction, she could not resist meeting him clandestinely.

"Your Grace?" she gingerly called through the door.

He opened it, and she was greeted to his warm and inviting study. "Evening, Peytra, come in." His voice seemed oddly flustered. "I was thinking of perhaps playing a game. Have you ever played Jrenznik?"

"Yes. My father taught me when I was young. I've even made pieces for a set at home."

"Ah, well then, I hope you'll indulge me." He gestured towards a pre-set board at a corner of the room near the fire. He'd set up two chairs across from each other. She sat down, and he pushed in her chair the way he might have for a woman of his same social standing. He asked her to roll and move first, and they began the game.

It was clear she'd been an experienced player by her first set of moves. This was enjoyable to Jors; she provided an unforeseen challenge. But he also found himself distracted by the way the firelight danced off her skin and the way she furrowed her brow before making a move. He was enjoying the sight of her as much as the game.

"Your Grace," she paused and remembered, "um, Jors, do Dukes always have to settle land disputes?" She moved a piece after interrupting the silence.

"We do when the nobles are in our protection.

The dispute is between a Marquis and Viscount, and it concerns a ten-mile stretch of riverbank between their two properties. Their families have intermarried, and recently, a common relative who owned the land passed away. Now comes the challenge of appeasing both parties while honoring the law." He made his move and looked back at her. A ringlet that fell along Peytra's brow gave him pause. Seated as she was, her arms casually wrapped to her, she looked like a classic portrait.

"Couldn't you just split the land in half?" She rolled, moved, and looked back at him.

"That would make simplest sense, but the two parties are consistently on the brink of warring. It'll be better and fairer for me to give them both an audience and allow each to make their case before presenting a decision. That is the business of power; to maintain it, I must earn it. It's better done with hearings than force, in my opinion." He moved, then leaned back and looked at the board and at her.

She rolled her dice and noted the low balance. "That sounds understandable. Is Marcus actually good at contracts?" She moved.

Jors was caught off guard. He took a longer look at her trying to detect her motive for the comment. Had she detected his attraction to her, and therefore his jealousy? Was she using that as leverage in their game? Or was it simply an innocent query? Jors couldn't read her, and this was both frustrating and beguiling to him. He moved. "He'll do in a pinch, so long as he doesn't flirt too heavily with the Viscountess or the Maquis' mistresses."

"You may want to bring a muzzle then."

Jors let out a loud laugh, and she couldn't help but join him. "I may need you to make one out of stone just to be sure."

"I'll do it for free as long as he has to wear it all the time."

"I see he's made an impression on you."

"He's just shameless." She rolled her eyes and shook her head. "Is he like that with everyone?"

"Aye, since we were children. He especially loves telling me about who on my staff he has, umm," Jors cleared his throat, "he has, enjoyed the company of." Perhaps this would dissuade her from any affection she may have for him.

"He has no problem telling everyone that," she said sardonically. She finally moved. It seems both of them had forgotten about the game.

They continued their game with restless chit chat. The game ended with no clear winner. Peytra found herself falling asleep in the chair and excused herself for the evening. He escorted her back to her room, silently sneaking in the hallways like they were in trouble. At her doorway, she abruptly turned to him and said, "While you're away, you can write to me if you want." Then, suddenly realizing what she had proposed, she turned and opened her door, spilled out, "Goodnight Jors," and ran inside her room, locking the door.

The Duke lingered for a moment outside of her doorway, a palm pressed against the wood wishing he could reach out to her. Wishing to take her with him when he left in the morning. But he was caught with the impropriety of his status. And he was caught with the knowledge that his body would have to remain a mystery to her.

Peytra leaned against the door. Why had she said that? To a duke of all people? She hadn't been around nobility long, but from what she'd heard when she was younger and what she'd picked up from the castle, their interaction was odd. Nobles weren't supposed to fraternize with her as much as this one was. He was strange, even for someone high born. At the same time, she pitied him. To live closed off from everyone because he'd been mutilated years ago. That type of life must be lonely. She looked down at her hands and wished desperately that she had hands that could sculpt him a new body, or reshape the his like clay. To ask him to write was bold, impetuous, and painfully like her. Peytra had become accustomed to him in a way that was new and frightening. And yet, she wanted dearly to keep exploring that feeling.

CHAPTER 8

The summer days had grown hot and so had the castle. Outside, the steam rose up in clouds from the nearby rivers and blanketed the area in humidity. The heat and steam was such that the stone walls could not protect against it, and thus the castle became like an incubator. The staff spent their days half-dressed and going about their work lazily, as the heat had sucked out their zeal.

The worst place to be was the kitchen, by far, so much of the cooking was moved outdoors when possible. The coolest places to be were the hallways in which Peytra was finishing the archways. One set led into the grand ballroom, where the high ceilings gilded with cool gold and marble chilled the air – it was the most pleasant of places to be. Since there wasn't as much food to prepare as people were away, Peytra often found herself in the company of Kori, Gani, and sometimes Una. They would sit on the scaffolding as she worked for an hour or so and gossip or tell stories. This would have been more pleasant had Peytra not already been so agitated

MASK OF THE NOBLEMAN

from the heat. But truly, she was more upset about the fact that the Duke had yet to write her. She had allowed herself to be vulnerable and felt faulted for it.

On this day, the girls were noting the stone sigils on the archways and trying to remember the different families and the meaning behind the sigils.

"I think that's a duck, right?" said Gani, squinting.

"No. No. That's a goose. Means fidelity," Kori replied, snacking on a grape.

"You think everything means fidelity. That's what you said about dogs, mice, and rabbits," Gani replied.

"What can I help it if royals like to be fidelation?" Kori paused and squinted, thinking, "Fidelarious? Fidlium?"

"Fidelitous," answered Una, stealing a grape.

Gani tapped Peytra on the back of her leg. "Eh, Peytra, what is that? A duck or a goose?"

Peytra stopped and turned with her hands still in their place to look in the direction Gani was pointing. She squinted. "Duck. You can tell by the beak."

"Told you," Gani said with a gloating smile.

"Ah, then that's the Pindell clan. They're known for their feather trade," said Una.

"Ahhh," the others said in unison.

There was a lull for a bit, then Peytra interrupted it. "Why a bear?" She wiped her brow.

"You mean for the Ameros family sigil? That's a long story," said Una, ready to start a long discussion.

"No," Peytra interrupted, "for his mask. Why

77

does the Duke use a bear for his mask instead of a face?"

"He used to," said Kori, "but it just looked odd and frightening. Gods, remember, Gan, when he first tried out all those masks. They were just so odd and uncomfortable. Made everyone frightened of him. Someone suggested he tried something not so human, and I think it works better that way."

"Oh yes, he first wore a black hood after he'd been burnt and then commissioned all these masks from all over. Some better than others. Someone sent that one, and it worked best, and he's kept it since," added Gani.

Una nodded. "I think he's come to think of it as his face."

Peytra mulled over this for a moment, and her heart felt for the Duke and his scarred face.

"Luckily, he makes sure that the annual ball he throws is a masquerade. Think you'll be done by then, Peyt?" said Kori.

"The what?" Peytra was blindsided.

"It's in a few months' time. It's something all rich people do," said Gani.

"Well, really, it's both his birthday and the same time those under him swear fealty," added Una. "It's a grand affair and a pain in all our arses."

"All the nobles beneath him are required to come, and sometimes his relations visit as well. Two years ago, the King showed up," said Kori.

"And these doors have to be finished by then?" asked Peytra, beginning to panic.

"I doubt it. This seemed like a sudden project.

He never consulted me on getting a new carver," said Una. "If you'd like, I can write to him and ask?"

Peytra almost answered that she would do that, but it still seemed like a secret worth keeping. "Yes, please. I'd appreciate it."

Just then a page walked in with mail for Una. He'd also been searching for a Peytra Sike in the castle and was told she'd locate her. Peytra took her letter and retired to her room, saying she wanted to reply if it was urgent. She gleefully ran to her room and lit a candle in the heat of it. She lay in her bed and ripped it open to read. It began:

My Dearest Peytra,

The talks here have stalled as neither party wishes to yield their claim nor compromise. It's been rather frustrating and has delayed my visit much longer than I would have preferred.

I never thought to ask, but do you like the seaside? The weather is rather pleasant, and at very least, the seaside is calming. I think you would like it here. In the morning, the sun crests over the water and lights the entire world up in gold for a few moments. At night the moon is reflected over the water, and one can scarcely tell the difference between the sky and ocean.

There is also an interesting little tradition of boat races here that I think you should find entertaining. They make small schooners that they race two at a time. The locals carve their own mastheads for their boats, which are also part of a contest. I would suggest you join such an endeavor – but I fear your gifted hands would make fools of them all. I would very much like to bring you here someday, to show you all this in person.

How is home? I hope you are well, and if it should please you, I look forward to a return letter.

In Care
Jors

Peytra read the letter. Then re-read it several more times. She was shocked by the informality of it. That he had begun it with "my dearest" had made her heart jump in such a way she could not suspect it. Little did she know that he had agonized over that line for over a week before sending it. That he wanted to take her somewhere, that he wished to be with her created a small pocket of warmth inside her chest, unaffected by the summer heat. She took the rest of the afternoon to write her reply.

My Dearest Jors,

The weather has turned hot, and the castle has decided to burn us all with it. But we are all well aside from that.
As for the ocean, I've never been. My oldest sister went with her husband once. She brought me back a seashell sand dollar which I keep with me. But I think I should like to see it. If boat races are anything like cart races, I'm sure I'd enjoy it. I'd also love to see the mastheads and the way they are done.

As for the hearings, I'm sorry things have stalled. It's a pity because we at the castle miss all of you and would like to have you all back. I miss our late night chats, and this place seems a little empty. Perhaps you could tell them that you'll give the land to a third party to prompt them to compromise? I don't know if that will help. If they're going to act like children, I don't see a reason to not treat them as such.

Anyway, I hope you are in good health and finding ways to enjoy yourself. I look forward to your letter or to your return.

In Wait
Peytra

She sent it off early the next morning. When the heat began to make her upset, she would return to the letter she'd received, and it would alleviate the discomfort.

※

The middle of summer was the worst for sleep. The heat stayed in the stone, and many found themselves drenched in sweat in the middle of the night. It made for odd and vivid dreams. One of these nights, Peytra found herself in the most vivid of nightmares.

In it, Peytra was walking along a sandy riverbank. A very large swan, almost Peytra's size glided by. She was not afraid but comforted by the bird which approached her. It used its beak to point at something at Peytra's feet. It was the small carved bear Peytra had made. Instinctively she knew to throw it, and mid-air it turned into a large, black bear that looked over at her. The bear turned and began to walk towards the tree-line of a forest, and Peytra followed it.

. . .

The bear gradually picked up speed until they were running through the trees before it jumped and disappeared. In its place was a man with his back turned towards her. He wore a thin white shirt and black pants that hugged a muscled figure. He had long, red-tinted blonde hair that curled naturally at its ends. When he turned around, she saw blue eyes that she had looked into before, on a face that was unblemished and perfect. He smiled and breathed her name excitedly, "Peytra."

"Jors," she breathed. *This must be what he would have looked like if he hadn't been burnt* she thought.

He ran to her, lifted her up, and spun her around. He then took her face in his hands, cradling her jaw within them, and kissed her deeply. "I'm so happy you're here. I've been wanting to dream of you," he said, grabbing her hand.

"Dream of me?" She followed him as he walked through the forest.

"Yes, I know you're just a dream, but this is still a joy," he said, smiling at her.

"Yes, but it's my dream. At least I think?"

He was all joy still. "Maybe we were to dream of each other, and the gods sought to put us together."

She was still confused but also filled with happiness. For once, she got to see him behind everything, and she felt that she was seeing him the way he saw himself.

. . .

They reached their destination, a small waterfall shrouded in greenery. He turned to her, taking her hands in his. "Peytra, do you trust me?"

She eyed him suspiciously. "Yes…"

"Then follow me!" He dove off the waterfall and plummeted into the pool below.

"I can't swim!" she called.

"It's a dream! You can do anything in a dream! And I'm here! Trust me!" Even from this distance, his smile was beguiling.

Peytra gathered her fear and felt it melt away for a moment. It was only a dream. She jumped and fell feet first into the water. For a moment, she was enveloped, but he pulled her up to him. She began to float on the water. It was invigorating. They joked, they laughed, they kissed. All the inhibitions that Peytra had were gone with the notion that this was all fantasy. This dream version of Jors was everything she'd ever thought he could have been, with clean chiseled features, an expressive face, and a muscular frame. They got to the shore and walked along the trees.

It was blissful until Peytra kicked something with her foot and bent to pick it up. It was the Duke's mask with a large crack along the face. She heard a scream from behind. Then "No! Don't look at me!" But it was too late. Peytra had turned, and there was Jors, engulfed in a black and green flame. "NO!" Peytra screamed, stepping towards him, but he began to melt and dissolve into a black and green puddle.

"SAVE ME PEYTRA! FIND ME!" were his last words.

Peytra woke up screaming and grabbing for her sheets before she realized it had been a nightmare. Miles away, Jors Ameros awoke from the same nightmare. He'd had that dream so often before, it was now routine. Except this time, he hadn't been alone. He went to the vanity and washed the sweat from his face and wished desperately that, even though it had been a dream, that he had at least kissed her once more.

CHAPTER 9

The post came early in the morning. Una was glad to inform Peytra that the arches and doors did not need to be finished by the time the ball was to happen. Then she handed Peytra the letter addressed to her. Peytra absconded to her room and read the note in secret.

My Dearest Peytra,

I do not know which will reach you first – this letter or myself. We are to leave today, and should all go well, I will be home in two days' time. I have you to thank for helping us to reach an accord as it was your advice that spurred the two parties to action. It worked brilliantly, and I am extremely grateful.

As for the temperature, I am quite sorry if it is making you miserable. I do have a summer residence in the north that tends to be cooler. It has fallen to disarray from my neglect, but perhaps it can be restored in time for next year's summer. Then we could all stay there for a few months.

Otherwise, I look forward to returning home and resuming our evening meetings. I hope you've been sleeping well.

Affectionately,
Jors

Peytra pondered over the letter. How did he know about her nightmare? She brushed it from her mind and resumed her excitement. *They'll be home soon!* she thought. *He'll be home soon!* But the image of his body melting was stuck in her mind.

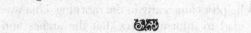

It was dinner time when the retinue came in. They shuffled into the servants' kitchen with one page telling Gani to send up a meal – there would be no formal dining that evening. Although they were exhausted, they were full of cheer. Hue, Georgie, and Marcus went on and on about the scenery. They spoke about the beer, the ocean, the boat races. Georgie and Marcus went on and on about the women. Some presented gifts. Hue gifted Una with a glass-blown quill, stating simply that he felt it would work well while she was writing the ledgers. She was touched.

"I guess that dispute was solved then? No problems?" Peytra asked.

Hue, Georgie, and Marcus lit up. "Oh, there were problems," said Georgie with a giant smile. "But the way His Grace solved them, that– *that* was a work of brilliance."

"I've never seen him that scheming, but my Gods, it was something to see," Hue added.

"What happened?" Peytra asked.

"Well," Georgie started while leaning in and dropping his voice, "the talks had completely deteriorated. Now anytime they met in a room, the Marquis and Viscount, they started bickering."

"Turns out both had an almost equal relation to the deceased owner. They tried arguing over status, precedence, and all that," said Hue.

"Well, one afternoon, His Grace approaches me and tells me to, um, well, to try to engage the Viscountess and the Marquis' mistress in charming conversation," said Marcus with a devious smile. "Of course, I was only happy to oblige. Especially with the Viscountess."

"Let the muzzle off the dog..." mumbled Peytra.

"What was that?" asked Marcus.

"Nothing. You were saying," said Peytra.

Georgie continued. "One afternoon after Marcus had been let loose, the Marquis and Viscount resumed their fighting and well..."

"The Duke interrupted them and shouted them down. Told them that if they could not come up with a peaceful accord by the next day noon, he would gift the land between them to Marcus," said Hue.

"And all they had to do was look at the way their women were looking at Marcus when they promptly stopped their bickering and got to work. They reached an agreement before the night was through," said Georgie, punctuating his laugh with a loud clap.

"Ah, what could have been," said Marcus, a wistful look on his face. "Me, with my own land near the sea, some beautiful ladies nearby. Ah, but was not meant to be."

"You should have seen their faces; the Marquis looked like he was about to fall out of his chair. It was glorious," said Hue.

Peytra smiled. The Duke had taken her suggestion and improved it. She was proud.

"His Grace was in a hurry to come home, though. I would have liked some more time to sit by the sea," said Georgie.

"Perhaps he was simply homesick." Marcus eyed Peytra with a knowing look.

※

The rest of an evening was a flurry of activity. Peytra had never heard such a string of curses as Gani finding herself in the position of making more than thirty meals after dinner. "And they all eat like horses!" She barked through the kitchen, more at Kori and the other kitchen maids, but also to let some of the guards know that she was irked at their insistence on eating.

Una found herself compelled to put together briefings, even though, in her words, "The Duke is most likely too exhausted to read such things right now, but I wouldn't be so good at my job if I didn't at least do this!" She was also, Peytra suspected, excited to use her new glass quill.

Late in the evening, after assisting Gani in Kori in the kitchen, Peytra sat in her room, brushing her hair. She had just washed with the washcloth and water bowl in her room. In doing so, she wiped away many of her anxieties of the past few weeks. She stood naked in her room, acutely aware of her body's dips and crevices. She applied fingertips of oil to her scalp and brushed it out to smooth the black tresses that were naturally curled from the long braid she wore and pinned each day. She lifted the small hand mirror to her face to view a brow free of the day's sweat and work. Then she pulled back the mirror to see more of herself. She noted how her long hair fell down attractively over her shoulders. Then she rubbed the remaining oil onto her feet, hands, and skin and wiped the excess off with a cloth. She felt that her body was new and changed in a way she could not quite understand.

As she put her underdress over her head, she heard a shuffling from above and knew that the Duke was in his study. She was emboldened not to wait for him to find a more obvious signal. She put on a thin kirtle and contemplated quickly braiding her hair. Then she remembered how alluring she looked at that moment and decided against it.

As quiet as a mouse, she snuck up to the study. Before she could knock, the door opened before her. The Duke stood there in silence. For a moment, Peytra worried that she had disturbed him or intruded on something private. What she could not see was how he held his breath at the sight of her. He clutched the door, resisting the urge to take her into his arms.

"Evening, Peytra," he said with as much forced decorum as he could muster. "I was just on my way to see if you'd like to join me." Jors noted that he'd never seen her with her hair down and was distracted by its allure. He opened the door further and beckoned her to come in.

Peytra walked gingerly into their private sanctuary and took her typical seat. "Did you have a lovely trip?"

"It was mostly business with little time for leisure," he coughed awkwardly. "Did you, um, receive my correspondence?"

"Yes! I looked forward to your letters." There were hundreds of questions running through her mind then, and she did not know which to ask.

"Well, as I recall, you stated that the only keepsake you had from the seaside was a shell. I decided to keep up the tradition. For you," and he pulled a small box from a drawer in the side table. Within the box was a small, spiraled shell on a chain.

"It's...gold?"

"Yes, that is a local tradition. They melt gold coins given to the Sea God's temple and dip shells into them, then sell those shells to pilgrims. It has to do with a local story."

"Which story?"

"A local folktale involving a sea-woman, the god of the Sea, and a poor fisherman. Would you like to hear it?"

"Well, I do like a good story," she said, trying her best to be coy.

He cleared his voice and began. "I'll try to tell it the way I heard it. Long ago, there was a poor fisherman who lived in the village of Relinki when it was still small huts along the ocean and the people made their homes on the boats. He was young, kind, and hardworking. But above all things, he was deeply in love with a maiden of the village, and she had fallen in love with him. They were set to be married when she drowned in a strange accident and died when the moon was full. Grief-stricken, the fisherman remembered an old legend that Aridion, god of the sea, could bring to life those that had drowned on the full moon if he was gifted a thousand seashells. The fisherman scoured the shoreline, not sleeping nor eating until he had collected a thousand seashells.

"When he had the shells gathered, he took her body and the shells to the sea and begged Aridion to bring her back to life. Aridion heard the fisherman's prayer and granted it. But he brought the maiden back to life as a fish-tailed sea-woman. For a time this was fine, the fisherman spent his life on his boat out at sea with her. Yet, as the days went on, the fish maiden cared less and less for coming to the surface. The rest of her began to grow scaled and fish-like until she seemed to not care for her former love. The fisherman prayed and prayed to Aridion to make her human again. Aridion said he would, but only if the fisherman brought him the shell of the great golden clam that lived at the bottom of the sea.

"By this time, the maiden had disappeared into the deep ocean, preferring to spend her time among the corals and fish. He prayed and dived into the ocean, searching and searching for the great golden clam. Swimming without food, fresh water, or sleep for seven days and seven nights."

"He found it, right?" Peytra deeply felt for the fisherman.

"Sadly, no. A storm came, and he also drowned. They say, however, that Aridion took pity on him and brought him back as a fish-tailed sea-creature. Now the fisherman and the maiden swim the oceans together. That is why the villagers dip their shells in gold and wear them when they go out to sea. They hope that, should they also drown, Aridion will take that as payment and spare their lives."

"At very least they have a happy ending," said Peytra. "I mean, well, both were changed, but at least they got to be together. Then again, I think most of these stories are just that – stories."

"Ah, so you don't believe in the gods?"

"Well, I do, but I don't think they interact with us the way they did in the very old times," Peytra said somewhat carelessly. When she realized what she had admitted, she began to panic. "I mean, well, ummm…"

Jors held up a hand to calm her. "Don't worry, you'll not face religious persecution here. I care not what you or anyone else here believes. Some of my staff here are not even of our faith. Kori and Gani, for example, are Uminites."

"They worship the feline god?"

"Yes. I'm not here to judge anyone of their piety."

"Speaking of which, I was wondering something. What did you do with the Fregh statue? I hope you still enjoy it."

"Very much so. I had it placed in the temple here."

"There's a temple here?" Peytra asked. And then she thought of all the minor chastisements her mother had written to her in their correspondence about making sure she was praying regularly. She had forgotten the statue had been bought for the temple here.

"Yes, it's at the northwest corner."

She made a distinctly quizzical face, both from guilt at her mother's words echoing in her head and for not knowing about the place where she was living.

"Would you like me to show you where it is?" he asked.

"Now? Wouldn't we be seen?"

"Not necessarily. Let me show you," he said with youthful excitement in his voice.

The study had a small secret passage located to the back corner opposite the fireplace. The passage forked a few feet in, he explained. One path led to his quarters and then on to the quarters that were for the lady of the house. The other path led to an underground tunnel that let out at the temple. This tunnel was constructed by his predecessors, he said, as a result of peasant rebellions all over the country. Or at least that was the excuse. He believed the real purpose was to sneak in his great-great grandfather's mistresses, one of whom famously had a residence less than half-a-mile from where the tunnel let out.

Perhaps he was purposely, intuitively distracting Peytra from her discomfort. The passage was exceedingly claustrophobic with tiny leaned-in walls and no lighting. Instead, they had only one lit candle he had brought. His black clothing made it difficult to differentiate his person from the darkness that surrounded them, and she found herself accidentally pressed against him at several intervals. On the one hand, this was extremely improper; on the other, she was comforted by the warmth and shape of him.

Jors could hear her heavy breathing and noted how frightened she was. He took her hand to both guide and comfort her. He noted how those skilled hands fit so well into his, but could not find the right words to say it. Instead, he guided her, relishing the physical closeness they had at the moment.

They reached a small doorway, which he pushed open. He told her to wait as he lit up the temple, and one by one, torches sprung to life. The temple was taken care of by a priestess and her husband under the Duke's salary who lived in residence close by. It was open to all castle residences and the locals.

As the place was lit up, Peytra noticed that the door they had come through was actually a false wall. Now that it was clearly lit, she could tell that the temple was about half the size of the one back home, but it was also in better condition. Looking up, she noted that the high ceiling was done in the old style, with a colored glass that bordered all the sides. Even now, with just the starlight to illuminate it, she could see how the glass made the light into richly hued tones that danced on the white marble.

Around the temple, there were ten-foot tall statues of the eight main gods. Their stylization was a hodgepodge – newer ones had replaced decayed ones. They were carved, painted, and gilded wood, and she stood in awe of them. In their varied ages and styles, she could see the evolution of her trade in a way she never could before. The blocky, stylized edges of the classic era, the skillful flourishes of the old masters, and the intricately patterned edges of her own time. The newest statue was that of Fregh, and Peytra recognized the hand right away.

"Tochtem made her, right?"

"Correct," he answered. He'd been lost in the revelry of watching her as she had studiously and excitedly examined the statues. Jors could tell that she was enchanted with the place, and his heart leapt at seeing her enthralled. But now he was back at entertaining her. "My mother served as the model."

"I can tell, those features, they are almost the same as the portrait. She really was quite beautiful." Peytra paused at the quiet and realized that bringing up his mother may be a reminder of painful memories. For a moment, it crossed her mind how cruel fate had been. That his mother should be struck by lightning, the great fire of the sky, and that he should have been burnt before his prime. These were things that she desperately wished to make better for him. She examined him for a moment, trying to read his body language for some indication of his feeling.

"Let me show you where we've placed your statue." He led her to the back walls where there was row upon row of alcoves used for offerings and reliquaries to both the major and minor gods. There, in a central one, was her statue in an alcove that had a metal shell. The light of the torches was reflected by this metal, and it lit up the statue as if it itself glowed. Peytra could not help but be proud of this display. That her work was displayed in the same room as great artists before her time and could be viewed by any worshiper filled her with an immense feeling of pride.

Just then, it dawned on her the job she'd taken on these past months. Her archway and door carvings were going to be part of a building hundreds of years old. Her art would have a legacy beyond her death and hopefully would last lifetimes from them. Perhaps like Tochtem, she would be an artist with a name.

Peytra felt very faint just then. "I think I need to sit down." Jors looked back at her face, which had suddenly grown pale, and began to panic. He led her to a seat near the center, where worshipers would typically sit and pray to the gods. Jors tried to keep his voice calm and even as he searched for some water around the temple, or something else for her to drink. He feared that all the excitement of the evening had made her ill. He ran around the back ends of the temple with a guilty conscience. When he returned, he put forth a voice of reassurance. "I could not find water, but this sacrificial port wine may help. I believe it's meant for Umilri, god of health, which is appropriate." He poured her a small glass and put it gingerly in her hands, then sat down next to her.

Peytra looked at the goblet with curiosity then downed the port in one go. The liquid warmed her chest, and she looked back at Jors, whose blue eyes were squarely focused on her. *He's so tall*, she thought, *and so kind. Look at him, worried about me and caring for me.*

And he never asks for anything, and he wants to give me everything.

Maybe it was the wine, or the warmth of the night, or the fact that she had just realized how deeply she'd missed him, but she decided to ask for something that she'd been desperate for. She took a moment to gather her words. "Jors. When I was younger, there was a man in the village who had a horrible accident. He'd burnt half his face with lye, even lost an eyeball. Yes, some of the villagers teased, but he still went on to marry and be accepted by everyone. And I never thought anything of him. I never thought of him as different.

"What I mean to say is, you've given me so much, and I have no right to ask for anything. But will you let me see you? I don't care what's happened to you, I'll still feel the same about you. I just, please, Jors, let me see you."

Beneath his mask, he smiled in spite of himself. Jors was touched by her sentiments. There still remained the ache in the knowledge that no matter what he wanted, he could not show her his skin. He thought for a moment of how to explain this to her, knowing that no explanation he could give would be satisfactory. Then he thought of another way to give her what they both wanted.

His eyes locked with hers. "Peytra. Do you trust me?"

She thought through his question, one which could leave her vulnerable, but she knew deep in her being what her answer was. She squared her jaw. "Yes."

He took out a handkerchief and asked her to close her eyes. She acquiesced, and he gingerly tied his handkerchief around her eyes, making a blindfold. Peytra had a combined feeling of nervousness and excitement, as every inch of her skin seemed to burst with electricity. She breathed in deeply, trying to calm her quick-beating heart. There was a ruffling sound, and she heard the distinct sound of a wooden object clicking against the bench. He'd removed his mask. She instinctively bit her lip.

A moment later, he took her hands in his newly ungloved ones. For the first time, Peytra felt the Duke's skin. His palms felt warm and rough against her fingertips. As much as she was exploring this new sensation, he was reciprocating. He rubbed his thumbs on the back of her hand between her thumb and forefinger. Then wound his fingers between hers before bringing them up to his face.

With her sense of sight still deprived, she used her hands to "see" his face, painting a portrait in her mind. She began at the base of his chin, tracing her fingers along his jawline, which was squared and centered on a prominent, dimpled chin. He had a day's worth of stubble, which went upwards to hollowed cheeks. She felt his nose, a straight line downwards that ended with naturally widened nostrils. Her hands approached his brow and hairline. Her hands stroked his shoulder-length, waved hair away from his face. She returned, feeling his eyebrows and eyelids, then working her way back downwards.

She pulled her hands for a moment in hesitation, he pulled them back, and she traced his nose down to his lips. With her forefingers, she traced the outline of them, and then with her thumb, felt the center of his bottom lip. His lips were thin but plumped in the middle. She felt his hot breath on the tip of her finger, and it burned pleasantly.

Suddenly he grabbed her left hand with his right and pressed her palm to his lips and kissed it. She gasped and felt a shock run through her entire body, ending at the tips of her toes, which curled in her shoes. For a moment, he sat there, breathing and rubbing his face into her palm.

"Peytra?" he asked suddenly. His voice was clear and strong, no longer bound by the mask he wore.

"Yes?" she replied, somewhat weakly.

"Do you trust me?"

"Yes." She tingled all over with excitement.

"Then give me this gift."

Before she could reply, he had his hands at her jaw. Tilting her face a little higher, he placed his lips on hers. The kiss was deep and long. Impossibly, it felt both wonderfully new and strangely familiar. His face bore down on hers, their breath intermingling as his lips folded around hers. He moved to cup her head in one hand and wrap his other arm around her, holding her close. She wound her arms around him to press herself against him as well. She could feel the beating of his heart in her chest.

Jors took her in. The softness of her skin, the smell of her, and the way in which her body moved up against his. He wanted so desperately to show himself to her, to reveal the face he kept hidden. This was as close as he could safely get, but it was a moment he felt he could cherish.

At that moment, she didn't care what he looked like. Peytra decided that if she needed to, she would wait forever to see him with her eyes. As long as he needed her to.

CHAPTER 10

An affair is a curious thing, Peytra thought while she chiseled away at the door. It'd been over a week since their first kiss, and they'd taken to meeting every night since. Sometimes they talked as they did before, only with more openness and connectivity. Sometimes she blindfolded herself in anticipation of the physical closeness that they both deeply craved. Sometimes they held each other in silence just to take comfort in the nearness of one another.

Their days were the same as before. The Duke had his obligations running his lands while Peytra went about working on her art for him. They were cordial and professional whenever they met in front of others, but without prying eyes, they relaxed. There was the implicit understanding that whatever they had was new, but had to remain furtive.

She thought back to the courtships she had witnessed growing up. Those also seemed strangely secretive. Her brothers just seemed to be missing more often until they brought home their potential wives. It was the same with her older sister. There seemed to be a culture of secretiveness surrounding courtship. Or at least a culture of benign resignation to it. That one day, there was no relationship, but the next, there it was. Not that it really mattered in her case; she wasn't particularly thinking about the future of the affair as much as she was simply enjoying its presence. She pondered these things as Marcus came upon her.

"How's my favorite Birdie today?" he said, with a frighteningly dashing smile.

"Don't you have some work to do? Ever?" She switched tools.

"How can anyone work on a day like today!"

She shot him a look of contempt as he climbed up the scaffolding. He leaned against her door. "Woodpecker! Do you not feel it in your very flighty bones! Today is the last day of summer."

"Is it? I don't see what that has to do with what I'm doing here." Something hit her in the pit of her chest. This season had gone by too quick, like the heat dissipating into the air.

"Oh, Birdie, come join all of us out in the yard and grounds. Gani always makes a little picnic for us."

"I wasn't invited," she said dryly.

"Simple oversight. I'm sure they all thought you would just know. It's our own little tradition. Take your day of rest. Come and entertain me."

Peytra had noted how quiet the castle had been. "You're such a pain. How does His Grace deal with you?"

"You wound me, Birdie! And of course he puts up with me. I'm the closest thing he has to a brother."

"I have never felt more sorry for the man's lack of relations then."

"Well, it's true, we were born weeks apart, my mother was his nursemaid, my father his tutor. We looked so similar as children most thought we were twins. No doubt that if that nasty business hadn't happened to him, we'd probably be rivals. But as it happens, it's just my good looks vying for your affections."

She smiled in spite of herself.

"Ah, that smile means you'll join me, no?" He wiggled his eyebrows.

"Fine, but mostly because I could use a day without work." She also wanted to get away from her thoughts and just feel the last day of summer.

༒

It was as Marcus described. Much of the castle lay out on sheets in the gardens, feasting on the fruit on its last days of season. The children of the staff ran around their parents. Some maids played games of tossing rings, some guards tossed horseshoes. The day held its warmth, but breezes passed by teasing the oncoming autumn. Gani, Kori, Georgie, and Hue were laid out on an old blanket. Una was in a meeting with the Duke and a contingent of farmers from one region.

Marcus and Peytra joined them and their conversation, which mused on when was the last time Kori had washed this blanket, as well as the gossip everyone had picked up on.

Aside from procuring food, gossip was the trade of the kitchens. Whether it was soldiers, maids, pages, they all made their way to the kitchen at some point, and always feeling like they had to give something in return for their food, they exchanged rumors. With a grand ball less than a month away, there was plenty of gossip to be had. Gani and Kori were the distributors of this clandestine knowledge when their friends were close.

They started first with the guest list of who was coming and who was snubbing. Outside of those whose fealty was owed to the Duke, invitations went out to the adjoining nobility, most of whom were blood or legal relations. The guest list had increased steadily in the last few years as the Duke had worked to repair his family's reputation after his father's failings, which meant that once a year the castle became a chaotic metropolis, with nobles and their retinue coming by to make the castle their home for a few days. Gani and Hue were already dreading the preparations.

"He's really trying to get the King to come this year," said Georgie.

"That's the last thing I need. His Highness and his refined palette are a pain in my hide," added Gani with a sneer. Then she mumbled something along the lines of "allergic to potatoes my foot."

"Why do you say that?" asked Kori to Georgie.

"Because we've been having to coordinate a lot of letters between here and the palace. More than any other year," Georgie answered.

"You know, that makes sense. Malti said that the Duke wanted the large rooms on the East Wing opened and prepared. Said she had to chase a pigeon family out of one 'cause it's been so long they been there," said Kori.

"Is that strange? I mean the Duke wanting to bring the King, not the pigeons," asked Peytra.

Hue sat up and stretched, "I've worked as a guard for a lot of noble households and it isn't necessarily strange. Lots of nobles want to earn The King's favor and be invited to Court. Or they needed the King to solve a dispute on some matter. But the Duke's not one for court life, and he tends to keep his matters to himself. In that case, it is strange."

"He's probably doing it as a favor to the Marquis," interrupted Marcus. He was laid out on the blanket with his hands tucked behind his head. They all looked over at him, waiting. Finally, Peytra gave him a playful smack on his arm and commanded him to explain.

"Well, when we were with the Marquis Taunlik, his mistress, Ms. Ameli, and I had a number of, um, private conversations. Turns out they've been trying to marry for years, but the King has always denied their request and refuses their requests to meet at court. Maybe they hope our Duke could broker the conversation. I mean, Taunlik and His Grace get along alright," Marcus answered.

"Why don't they just marry?" asked Peytra.

"Nobles aren't allowed to marry outside of the nobility unless given permission by the King. Else he can strip their holdings and titles. Our King seems intent on keeping the noble bloodlines 'pure.' His father was less strict, even granted permission to the Lady Swan and Duke Willem retroactively," answered Hue.

"Well, why does it matter if they don't marry? I mean, why don't they just keep on as they are?" asked Peytra again.

"'Cause their children are bastards and have no claim to any titles or wealth or all that. It's worse for Ms. Ameli; the Marquis is still free to kick her out in order to marry, and she could end up destitute," said Marcus with a pause. "Well, maybe not destitute. They love each other deeply, and she could still make a living as she did before. She was an opera singer when she met the Marquis. Still can sing, and she still has her looks. But fear not, Peytra, her siren song did not enchant me when I had you to come back to." He rolled over and looked at her with large pleading eyes.

"Pity you didn't follow it out to sea and drown," said Peytra, which was punctuated by howling laughter from Hue.

At about that time, Una located them out in the yard and sat down with the group. She complained about the meeting, which was tedious reaffirmation of policy. Then she was tired from all the work she had to do in preparation for the ball and such. The group commiserated on this for a time when she introduced her own bit of gossip. "It doesn't help that the Earl of Retilk and his daughter, the Baroness, are coming a week early to stay and 'visit.'"

Marcus was truly engaged now. "Really? Well, that is curious." He smiled and rubbed his chin.

"Planning on setting your sights on the Baroness then? I feel sorry for the poor woman," Peytra said.

"Oh, no, no. I mean, by all accounts, she's a fine woman, but I believe this is a father's plot to marry off his daughter. Which is going to be quite entertaining to watch."

Una seemed to catch on. "You know that makes sense."

"What do you mean?" asked Peytra.

Kori interrupted, "The Earl is a cousin of the Duke, but he's been surprisingly warm to the Duke despite his father's, er, well, behavior. He's visited before. The Duke and the Baroness were friendly as youths as I recall. And she writes and visits from time to time."

"Yes, and the Earl's lands are mineral-rich, we have a very good set of trading agreements with them," added Una. "Perhaps he wants to cement that with a marriage? Is that what you mean, Marcus?"

"No," interrupted Gani. "He means the fact that she has laid with women." Kori gave Gani a knowing and furtive look.

"Exactly," said Marcus. "It was quite a scandal. There had been rumors for years, of course. But it all came to a head when a visiting noble, a cousin, walked in on the Baroness with two of her ladies-in-waiting in 'compromising positions.' Well, the cousin was simply shocked and left immediately, and naturally told everyone of the whole thing. Rumor has it that the ladies were dismissed, and now her father has commanded all ladies-in-waiting to wear veils lest she be tempted. Oh, as it's become increasingly hard to marry her off. Fools, though, that only makes her more attractive." He scratched his chin devilishly.

"Why does she have to be married off? And what does that have to do with the Duke?" asked Peytra.

"Well, she's the Earl's final heir. Her older brother's a notorious fool and philanderer. Really, the man makes my reputation look pious by comparison. It would be in the best interest that she produce a legitimate heir to their lands. Aside from that, given now the Baroness' own tarnished reputation, there are few choices they could find for a suitable husband. My guess is that they feel that since the Duke also lacks prospects due to his, well, condition, that he would be the best match."

"I wonder if we'll be getting a Duchess soon then," added Georgie.

"I don't know if he'd really do that, though," said Kori. "I've known the man since I was born. He isn't the type to bow to pressure. Or at least he always struck me as someone who was a bit of a romantic, like his mom. Or at least maybe he wants to get to know her."

"That's what the week is for," said Gani. "She has a week to charm him so they can announce an engagement at the Ball. Then he can't walk away."

"You are really quite frightening, Gani, when you want to be," said Georgie.

"Good, now you know not to cross me," she replied playfully.

"I guess you're right, though. And really, it must get real lonely for His Grace. Maybe desperation will win out, and we'll end up with a new mistress. I just hope she's nice," added Kori wistfully.

"Oh, I wouldn't bet too much on that. Seems to me the Duke has his eyes on other things," said Marcus cryptically and abruptly ended the conversation.

Late that evening, Peytra readied herself to go to the Duke's study. She often tried to pass the time while others went to sleep combing through her hair or the book she borrowed from the castle library. Tonight was similar but she was more restless than usual. She was distinctly agitated that the Duke had failed to mention the possibility of a bride, but then again there was always a small corner at her heart that mourned the affair even as it was happening. She'd never let herself think of what could be beyond the present situation. The day's discussion had eliminated the possibility that there would be anything long term, and while she felt as if she had come to terms with that early on, a part of her still felt wounded. It still felt used.

There was a rustle above as the Duke entered his

study. *Let him wait,* she thought, knowing that if she waited too long he would turn up at her door. *Let him come for me this time,* she thought defiantly. She was upset at herself for being upset. She knew what this was when it began, but perhaps she thought this small thing would be theirs forever. Truth is, she cared deeply for him. She loved how he was kind and encouraging. She loved that she could make him laugh and that they enjoyed a comfortable rapport. Then there was the physical. That for a man whose body was covered to never reveal even one inch of flesh, he was tender and instinctual. Or that his body felt strong and his skin, for what must have been scar tissue, felt remarkably unblemished.

Peytra could feel a heat rising in her chest at imagining the ways in which he held and kissed her. Thus far their interactions had been chaste and sweet. Sometimes she wanted more but also feared a transgression. She sat down on her bed for a moment. *Who am I? Am I a carver that happened to develop a relationship with the Duke? Or was that pretense to get me here? Am I a mistress who happens to carve? What do I want? Both?* she thought. And then she remembered the way his hands felt on her shoulders and the way his lips felt on her neck and that all seemed to become larger and smaller at the same time.

Maybe this is the beginning of the end. How fitting this comes at the end of the Summer. She played with the strings that tied her over-kirtle and debated just undressing and going to bed. Peytra wanted to go on like before in some ways. Continue the affair until she finished with the doorways and then leave with the memory of it. Keeping it as a little secret of her own for the rest of her life.

Peytra had been lost in thought that she hadn't noticed that the shuffling above had gone silent. Nor had she noticed the quick knock at the door. Just then the Duke rushed in and closed her door.

"Jors!" she almost squealed before he gently covered her mouth with a gloved hand.

"There were guards down the hall, and I would rather not compromise your reputation," he whispered. "We need to speak."

She nodded absentmindedly, fearing the worst. That this was the end, that she was to be sent away.

"I suppose you've heard the news," he said.

"Which news? That you're to have guests, or that the King may be coming?"

"The King is not yet guaranteed. As for the guests, well, the Earl is a necessary trading ally. But any speculation on an engagement or any such thing is simply that, speculation. Neither he nor Elle…"

"Elle?"

"The Baroness. We were childhood friends. Well, neither have ever raised a proposal as a possibility to me in any correspondence. You'll imagine my surprise when Marcus came by to congratulate me on my upcoming nuptials. I first thought he was referring to us until he mentioned the Baroness by name."

Us. I didn't know there was an "us," she reflected.

"But, Peytra, I want to make something abundantly clear. I do not plan on entertaining an idea of marriage between myself and the Baroness. I have no intention of courting her or being courted and I wanted to reassure you of that." He took her hands in his own gloved ones. It was clear he was agitated and insecure.

She closed her eyes and reflected on the situation. She tried to think the way a more court-savvy person might. "Well, wouldn't it be an advantageous marriage? A secured trading partner and a possible heir to your place."

"I have no intention in upkeeping a loveless marriage that is frighteningly common in people of my station. Peytra, I…" He got up to pace. "I was alone for a very long time. I kept myself on a path on rebuilding the titles my father had destroyed. On being what was responsible and necessary to the position. Years ago, I gave up on the possibility of solving the problem that was." He gestured towards his body. "And then, *then* I saw you in that little toy shop and you looked at me, and my Gods, Peytra, you didn't look at me like a monster or as some mysterious, frightening noble. No, you looked me in the eye like a person. Then I saw your art, that you could take something as formless as a block of wood and with your hands, with these hands, make that thing so much greater than itself. I hoped that you could do that for me, reshape me and my world. And you have."

"Jors…"

"What I want to say, Peytra, is that I find myself deeply in love with you and you alone." He kneeled at her feet and held her hands in his. "I cannot guarantee what will be tomorrow of us, nor how the pressures of my office will suffer this, nor that I know how to be a man that loves a woman, but I do."

Peytra could feel a beating in her chest. He didn't know how to love her, but she didn't know how to love in return. She knew that she longed to be near him when they were apart. She knew that her heart burst into joy when they were close. She knew that when he laughed, she felt that laugh come out of her chest. She also knew that she didn't care what he looked like beneath all the clothings and coverings. She would remain blind to it forever if need be, so long as he kept his body near her.

As an answer to him she tied a nearby handkerchief around her eyes, then feeling by her fingertips, she removed the mask he wore and kissed him deeply. They were still for a moment, enjoying the sweetness of it. Then she could hear him removing his gloves. He parted from her for a moment to remove his hood.

They kissed like before, but this time seemed different. There was a declaration there, that "love" hung silently in the air for them. But also this time, Peytra was ravenous and determined to enjoy this for what it was. She moved her hands slowly up his shirt, gliding her fingers across his tensed skin. She lifted his shirt off him, and although she couldn't see him, she was acutely aware that this was the most undressed the Duke had been in front of a person. She heard him briefly remove his boots, then he moved back to her. He answered her wandering hands with his own.

She grabbed his sides and pulled him towards her body as she fell back into her bed. He was now on top of her, hungry for her touch and affection. She squirmed playfully beneath him as he kissed and nibbled her ear. As she was moving she'd forgotten that her kirtle remained partially untied. One breast popped out which rubbed against his skin. She let out a sudden moan at the sensation. He looked down at it and cupped one hand on it. He pressed the nipple between his middle finger and thumb and watched as her face contorted with excitement. Then he kissed his way down to it, putting his lips on the center of her breast. She let out a small scream in pleasure. He continued to explore it, nibbling and sucking as she squirmed beneath him. Jors used his hand to free her other breast. Then he put his mouth on that one, using one hand to play with the other, while his free hand cradled her neck. He could see her from his angle, as she bit her lip and moaned with pleasure. She still had the blindfold on, and he desperately wished he could have removed it to look into her eyes.

The sensation was too much for Peytra, and she lifted her hips and pressed them against him. She wrapped her legs around him, and in a seamless movement, sat up and pushed him to sit on the bed. She adjusted herself such that she was straddling him. She had him pinned against the wall. She lifted herself up to kiss him and pulled more of her kirtle down to stroke more of her skin. Her hunger was great, but she didn't know what she wanted, only that she wanted pleasure of some kind between her legs. Even through his pants and her skirts, she could feel the firmness of his member. There was something instinctual to it, and she tilted her hips so that her part, through the fabric, pushed up against him. There was a sudden rush of pleasure, and she shook for a moment. Jors felt it as well and moaned.

"Peytra... I ...." he could scarcely breathe having her this close. He bit her shoulder, but she was relentless. She was searching for more, and she rubbed herself against him rhythmically. With each stroke, she could sense herself building up until she was going faster and faster. He desperately wanted to open her skirts and plunge himself into her, but he did not wish to push her. At the moment, it was difficult to concentrate with her body in front of him and the ways in which she moved against him. He wanted her to feel pleasure, and he would cater to her wants and needs. He bent forward to kiss her neck and continued to run his hands over her body.

The heat of his breath on her neck only increased her hunger, and she moved faster and faster. "Jors...I...I..." she huffed as her legs began to feel stiff. "I... don't... know... what's... happening... but ... I feel... I feel.... so good." She punctuated that with a moan.

"Peytra... I love you...do what you wish," and he kissed her hard on the mouth and pressed his member against her. She screamed in pleasure as the orgasm traveled from between her legs upwards. He felt her shiver, and that brought him close to the edge. But once wasn't enough. She wanted more, and she kept moving. He couldn't resist anymore either, and he too joined her second and third orgasm.

She collapsed against him as every inch of her buzzed with electricity. He laid them both down on her small bed, holding her against his chest. She curled into him like a cat, contented with what had passed and filled with a warm feeling of relief. He felt it too, intermingled with the fact that he had let her know he loved her. He'd kept it in his chest for what seemed like months and was relieved that he could at least show that part of himself to her.

"Jors," she whispered.

"Yes?" he kissed her forehead.

"Will I ever get to see you?"

"One day. I promise. One day." He seemed to think of something. "Peytra, may I ask you for something?"

"Yes, Jors." She nuzzled her head into the crook of his arm, still blindfolded.

"Will you make a new mask?"

She smiled. "Yes." She would give him the face she knew was there.

CHAPTER 11

The week went by in a whirlwind. It was soon announced that yes, the King would be coming to the castle. Gani was beside herself when she was notified that he would be sending his personal chef to prepare his meals as well. The guards and knights were compelled to rehearse and prepare their drills in honor of their guests. In the meantime, Peytra was finishing the archways to the Ballroom during the day, carving the Duke's mask in the evening, and rendezvousing some nights with him, yet they seemed to keep their contact deliberately chaste. There was a break in things when Peytra was invited by Una to get measured by the tailor. It seems the Duke planned to present her at the Ball as his artist-in-residence and was gifting her a gown. Una was also being fitted. It seemed that the managing castle staff were all expected to attend. Gani was invited but refused on the grounds that she did not trust Kori to not burn down the kitchen.

It was the middle of the afternoon when the Earl and Baroness arrived. Peytra was busy waxing one finished arch. But she heard all about the arrival from Kori, Una, and Hue over dinner. The way they told it, the Earl and Baroness both greeted the Duke warmly. Their retinue was small, consisting of a guard, valet, and two of her ladies-in-waiting. The ladies-in-waiting were truly peculiar in that, as rumor confirmed, they were veiled and covered completely from head to toe. The Duke was warm with the Baroness by all accounts, but none felt they were able to get a good enough look at her. It was then that a maid came to the servants' eatery in the kitchen searching for Peytra to let her know she'd been summoned to the salon and to follow forthwith.

She walked in behind the maid. Seated in the salon was the Duke on a long couch. Nearby was the Earl, a man somewhere in his fifties, reclined on a large wingback chair. He was shorter than she thought he'd be, with a squarish sort of face and trimmed hair. His dress was fine, if a bit too garish for Peytra's taste. On the other side, near to the Duke, was who must have been the Baroness. She was petite and curvaceous with ashen brown hair. She had deep bluish-green eyes framed into a squarish face. Peytra noticed that she had painted lips that enhanced their natural plumpness. In the background, her ladies-in-waiting stood like mysterious, veiled sentinels.

Peytra bowed towards each in turn. "Your Grace, Your Grace, Your Grace."

The Earl chuckled. "Good grief, girl, where did you learn your manners? It's 'My Lord' and 'My Lady' for the likes of us. How comical, 'Your Grace' for an Earl."

The Duke shot his face to the direction of the Earl. Before he could say anything, the Baroness spoke. "Oh come now, Father, that's nothing to chastise the girl for. I happen to find it charming. And really, Papa, isn't the greater sin to show hubris."

"Oh, you're right, my dear. My apologies, Elle."

Peytra was awed for a moment that this stranger had stood up for her in such a way. There was something about the way she took control of the discussion. She had presence added to by a melodious voice. Peytra stood a little straighter to stare down her competitor.

"Now, Peytra Sike, I believe that's what your name is, yes?"

"Yes, My Lady," said Peytra.

"Miss Sike, I have to apologize dearly for disturbing you. It's my fault you were pulled away from what you were doing, but I was anxious to meet the maker of those wonderful new archways I saw on the way in. I saw how wonderfully done they were from last year and begged Jors to introduce me to his new carver."

That's an odd pretense. Jors? She calls him by his first name? Peytra could feel herself turning red, but they must have read it as flattery.

"Oh, Miss Sike, I had no intention of embarrassing. I was just impressed with your skill. Our home region does not have this same rich history for woodwork, and so I am always marveled by it."

"Oh, um, thank you, My Lady. You are too kind." She bowed again. This was too much.

"Oh come now, dear, have a seat near me. Isadora, would you be a dear and get something for Miss Sike to drink." The Baroness gestured towards a nearby chair, and a veiled attendant brought a freshly poured glass of brandy. She then turned towards the Duke. "Jors, now you must tell me how you discovered her."

"Well, it was chance or fate, but I first saw her in her father's store. But it turned that she had submitted a sculpture to a contest the local village does.

It was quite impressive. That evening, due to a turn in the weather, we were meant to meet again, and I decided to hire her. She's been quite an addition even though she'd only been here a few months," the Duke said.

Peytra took a sip of the Brandy, and her ears burned. She felt that the Duke was trying to convey more about their encounters than he could do so openly.

"Tell me, Miss Sike, where did you learn your trade?" the Earl asked.

"Well, my father taught me," Peytra answered.

"Ah, so you have no formal training to speak of?" said the Earl.

Again, before Peytra could answer, "Oh, who cares of formal training. It's clear the girl has a gift! I've had fourteen years of formal training on the lyre and harp, and I still can barely carry a tune." The veiled maids chuckled silently at this. "See? Even Isadora and Mitchela know this is true. Oh gods, Jors, remember when we were children, and I did that horrible recital."

"You mean the time when two strings broke mid-concert, and you were so bad you didn't even notice the loss of those notes?" said Jors laughing.

"Yes! My tutor screamed at me for a half-hour after, and so I kicked him hard in the shin! See, Peytra, formal training can be a fool's errand," said the Baroness, smiling at her.

"I've just not had the opportunity yet," Peytra piped up to defend herself, "but my father taught me well, and he's a master craftsman of the guild as well."

At that time, Marcus entered the room, dressed in a finery he was rarely seen wearing on any other occasion. He gave a deep bow to both the Earl and Baroness, addressing them by their proper epithets.

"Marcus, my boy!" shrieked the Earl. "So good to see you. How have you been?"

"I've been excellent, My Lord, business is as it should. You are looking exceptionally fit. I see you are preparing to create a challenge for me among the ladies of the court!" The ribbing was clearly good-natured, but this only positioned Peytra into more outsider status.

"Oh, you know my days of chasing skirt are long behind me. I'm much too old for that. No, I've been taking in a number of hunts and sport these days," the Earl replied warmly.

"Well, it's doing wonders for you. And, My Lady, it's been much too long. I see you are still a vision as ever!" The Baroness nodded in appreciation, when Marcus spotted Peytra next to her. "And I hope you'll forgive me, but I see you've caught my little birdie in whatever trap you all are setting. I hope My Lady feels no offense, but I've fallen deeply for this little woodpecker."

Peytra was mortified as he pulled up a chair close to her. She didn't see the Duke clench his fist.

"None offense taken, Marcus, our affections would do the world no justice," the Baroness said playfully. "Wouldn't you say that, Jors?"

"Say what?" he seemed preoccupied.

"That any deep affection that Marcus may suffer for me or I for him would be a profound injustice."

"I think Marcus's affections towards anyone are bound to end in difficulties," the Duke answered sardonically. Peytra almost choked on her brandy.

"You wound me, Your Grace! Either way, what have you, My Lady, and my little birdie been discussing. No doubt gossiping about our upcoming nuptials?" Marcus said, turning back towards the women, hoping to goad some response.

"No, no, my dear sweet Marcus, we were simply marveling at this prodigy's skill." One of the veiled attendants silently placed a cup of tea in front of the Baroness. She took up the spoon for sugar and held it in such a way it triggered a sense in Peytra. Each finger positioned itself in such a way that denoted skill, poise, patience, and practice.

The Baroness must have caught her staring. "My evening cup. Can't sleep later without it." She smiled before placing the cup to her lips to take a luxurious sip.

"You're an artist," Peytra said with a bluntness she did not intend.

"Well, I do enjoy sketching. How did you know?" A sly smile crept across the Baroness's lips.

"The way you hold your spoon, it's like a pen or a pencil."

"How observant. Yes, I simply love to draw, but I've little ability to do so in the position I am in. I'm quite adept and enjoy drawing figures." She leaned in slightly. "I could draw you sometime if…"

Marcus let out a loud and deliberate cough interrupting their conversation and took a dramatic swig of his drink. "Now, My Lady, I forgot to ask what present costume would you be gifting us at this year's ball?"

"Yes! Well, this year I thought about what creature could possibly evoke my greatest assets and my painful weaknesses. Which should convey my mood for this season, and I tell you, Marcus, the question vexed me. I am not the graceful quiet of the deer, nor am I the belligerent crowing of a lark. Horse masks look simply beastly, and I am much too relaxed for that exertion. I did not wish to dress the same as I had in previous years, so a swan, a rabbit, and such were out. Then the answer revealed itself to me. It was the early afternoon, and I was walking back to my quarters when a cat crossed in front of me in the hall. It was a sign from above, I say. A house cat."

"A house cat? Really?" asked the Duke.

"Yes, Jors, a house cat. Think about it, I am as temperamental as a feline, I prefer things my way and do not take kindly to being ordered. My favorite things are to recline and be worshipped. Don't you think this is my best match?"

"Well, when it comes to temperament, I can see that," said the Duke in a friendly tone. Peytra looked at the Baroness as she reclined in the chair with her ornate gown. She seemed to make herself at home wherever she went. Her movement was indeed cat-like, as she drummed her fingertips on the edge of the armchair, not unlike a cat clawing at a tree to mark its territory. Peytra then got the distinct feeling that she was being played with, like a toy, or a mouse in the clutches of a feline captor.

"What about you, Marcus?" the Baroness asked, taking an indulgent sip and then nestling back. "Are you finally going to wear my suggestion?"

"What did you suggest?" asked the Duke incredulously.

"Oh, just that Marcus dress as something apropos to his person. Something that prances and enjoys flaunting its conquest." The Baroness smiled deviously. "A cock."

The Duke and Peytra laughed in unison. It was a perfect descriptor. Marcus, as was possible, pranced and paraded like a rooster, crowing about all his conquests. The Duke and Peytra looked over at one another, laughing like a secret was shared between them. She could see even from there the little crinkle that came up at the corners of his eyes. He loved watching her laugh, her laughing was always authentic and a full-bodied experience. It was deep and throaty and uncontained.

They didn't note the way that the Baroness, always observant, shifted her eyes between the two, keeping some secret knowledge to herself. She smiled, a devious smile to match Marcus's and let the two have a moment before intoning, "I feel you would look rather marvelous with a large crown of plumage bursting atop your head."

"My Lady, I would make the finest cock in history," Marcus replied with a smirk.

"He already thinks he is the finest cock in history," said Peytra, a little louder than she would have liked. They all laughed, but the Baroness laughed the most heartily at it, so much so that she wiped a little tear from the corner of my eye.

"My-my, Marcus, this birdie has teeth," she said. She gave Peytra a predatory look, but it was one that she couldn't quite read. *Does she know I'm her rival? Is it something else?* Peytra felt exposed, unsure of her position between herself, the Baroness, and the Duke. *Or does the Baroness simply like me as a friendly acquaintance?* While the Duke may have worn the mask, the Baroness seemed to have mastered that in her person.

It was then that they realized that the Earl had fallen asleep in his chair, which gave them all a good giggle. They continued the night, drinking, laughing, joking as friends. They talked about the balls of years pasts, the best costumes and the worst. They gossiped about this noble and that noble, the love lives and finances of the rich and powerful. It struck Peytra as peculiar, for a moment, that people like the Duke, the

Baroness, and even the Earl were seen as such fearful objects for many but, during this evening, were just as human as the lot.

Peytra found herself wandering the halls back to her room at the other end late at night. After a long string of banter, she had realized with a loud, impolite yawn just how tired she was and excused herself. Jors seemed ready to escort her to her room, but the Baroness tied him up in conversation. She'd had a bit too much brandy, and it seemed she had lost her way a bit. Outside she could hear the raging storm, the hurried rain beating against the stone walls of the castle. Every so often, the lightning would light up the now empty hallways. The workers were all in their beds, and the guards on duty were bearing down and securing the walls against the storm. The only sounds aside from the rain and thunder were those of Peytra's footsteps. To keep herself focused, she hummed a little tune, which echoed off the walls of the castle hauntingly.

Perhaps it was the brandy, or the lightning, or some combination of both, but at one point, Peytra began to see glowing footsteps in front of her that she couldn't resist following. Those steps led to a large mahogany double door. It was buttressed on both sides by ornately carved columns leading up to an imposing arch. In this dark, she couldn't make out the designs, but she felt the wood for a moment. It was old and scuffed from years of abuse.

Looking back at the door proper, the doorknob itself seemed to glow. Like with the glowing steps, her curiosity couldn't resist, and she gingerly opened the door. Squinting and searching around, she noted a candle on a side table. With a nearby match, she lit it. Peytra entered, closing the door behind her.

The small candle only lit about a few feet in front

of her. She called to see if anyone was there, and she was answered with silence. Towards her left were a large set of drawers and cabinets. Near to that was what Peytra gathered to be the largest bed she'd ever seen. It had four posts, each the thickness of her hips, which spiraled upwards. This led to a canopy a man-and-a-half's height off the ground. Her hand touched the sheet, and her fingers seemed to glide across the material. It was fine silk, so soft and smooth that one would feel like they were swimming to sleep in it.

Moving along to the other end, there was a solitary table and chair, an enormous fireplace, and another ornate cabinet. Something about the cabinet led her to open it up. Inside were stacks of books, each haphazardly placed. There were also boxes of odd-looking bottles and charms. She looked again to the books. They seemed to be in a language that Peytra could not read. It wasn't foreign, or it didn't seem so. In fact, the words looked desperately familiar for some reason. She could almost make out a few words. Something about "skin," "eyes," "blood," and "curses." Peytra puzzled over the texts. *Are these books on magic?* she thought. *Who in the castle practices magic? Whose room is this?*

She was given an answer when a familiar voice spoke her name. She turned around. There was the Duke, a candle in his gloved hand, but almost invisible as his dark clothing blended into the shadows behind him. Only his mask stood bright against the darkness.

"Your Grace," she said, suddenly uncomfortable for the trespass. She felt as if she had violated him and his privacy. For a moment, she forgot the closeness they already shared and was quick to return to formality. "I'm so sorry, Your Grace, I did not know this was your room."

"Peytra, were you looking for me?" he said, seeming more concerned than angry.

"Oh, I just, I was just lost and something, I um, I think it was the brandy."

"Well." He just looked at her for a moment. She noted that she was still holding his book, and she put it back in the cabinet.

"What language is that?" she asked abruptly, trying to break the very awkward silence.

"It's an older tongue, one in which our language is based in. Could you… read it?"

"Oh. No. I just thought it looked interesting. I'm sorry, Your Grace…"

"Jors."

She swallowed. "Jors. For looking through your things."

"It's fine, Peytra. I don't want to have secrets from you."

Her heart skipped a little. He was such a peculiar person. At once frightening, terse, and cold in public. Yet, when they were alone, he was freely affectionate. These moments of sincere vulnerability, this was the Jors she had come to treasure. "It still wasn't right of me, I know I wouldn't like it," she said, still hesitant to admit any feeling for him. "I should get to bed."

"If you'd like, I could escort you, or…" he halted, and then seemed to make a decision, "or you could sleep here. In fact, it would be my pleasure if you would."

She thought about the warmth of his body and the softness of those sheets. She thought about the way the brandy seemed to make her body so tired and less eager to leave. "I'd like that. I would like to stay." Peytra then began disrobing, her hands deliberately untying her frock and very conscious of his gaze. She was acutely aware of each motion she made and tried not to seem nervous. For all that they had done so far, things felt new. Peytra rationalized that it was the setting, that she had infiltrated a place that was truly his own.

He locked the door, perhaps, she thought, to keep a page or maid from barging in. She was now in only her underdress, and so she crawled into the bed and waited for him. She debated wearing nothing, but something in the air seemed chill. He passed her a handkerchief. Peytra felt her heart drop, realizing that he still didn't trust her enough to see him. Yet, she felt no right to protest and tied it around her eyes and lay down. She heard a familiar shifting, that of Jors removing his clothing and mask.

A moment later, she felt the weight of the bed shift as he climbed in with her. She suddenly froze, momentarily nervous about her position next to him. He wrapped his arms around her, and she realized that he was only in a nightshirt. She was caught between a sudden nervousness and one of desire. He felt her suddenly stiffen her posture and instinctively read to give her space. He really only wished to hold her. The day had been a trying one. Having to fend off the obvious advances of Ellotta and her father with any amount of grace and tact had been more exhausting than he anticipated. It also didn't help that he wasn't secure in Peytra's feelings for him.

Her eyes were covered by the blindfold, and he reflected on the tragedy of their partnership. He wanted to look into her eyes with his face uncovered, but could not. And she could not see his face outside the mask. Instead, she sat in the dark, out of compassion for him, their gazes always missing each other, passing each other by due to cruel circumstance.

While thinking about this, he absentmindedly ran a finger along the side of her jaw, admiring the shape of it. She seemed to shiver a bit but then turn her head closer. In the dim light of the last candle, he could make out her shape in the dark. He noted how her hip crested above her head as she lay on her side. He noted how her arms, typically muscular from her craft, softened as she lay down. Or how her hair, bent from the braid she wore, when let loose framed her figure with soft black waves. She was frighteningly talented, hardworking, and mercurial. He couldn't help but love her.

Jors ran his hand across her face and then his fingers through her hair. From this close, he could smell the oil she used for her skin, the wax for the woodwork, and the brandy she'd drunk that evening. His hand landed on the small of her back, and through her chemise, he felt the bend of her spine as it was bordered by muscle. She reacted to his touch by moving ever so slightly to his fingertips. He took that as his queue to press his hand on her back and shift her closer to him. Her body now touched his, and the heat of them both made the bed almost unbearably warm.

She could feel his arousal through the thin clothing they both wore, and while it unlocked an innate arousal in herself, Peytra was quelled from it with a lingering set of insecurities.

"Jors?"

"Yes?" he said, his thumb rubbing her back.

"What are those books?"

Now it was his moment for insecurity. "Old texts on lore. I'm searching for a solution to an old problem."

"Oh," she said, not sounding convinced. "They looked like spell books."

"I suppose that could be one way to look at them. That or religious texts, historical accounts, or other names. It's taken a number of years to acquire this collection."

"Are you… close to finding a solution?" She felt she already knew the problem, that he was looking for a cure for his condition. Or at least that is what she felt instinctively.

He breathed deeply and pulled her even closer. "There have been a number of years where I gave up on that possibility. I… I'd learned to live my life this way, with this system, and felt content to do it. But these past few months, meeting you, knowing you and falling in love with you prompts once again to search for it. Peytra, I don't mean to be cryptic. I don't want to secretive, but I…"

"It's fine, Jors. I trust you."

He took his thumb and stroked it against her bottom lip, feeling her breath on his fingertips. He then cupped her face in his hands and planted a soft kiss on her lips. They lay there for a moment, locked in the silent pose. They fell asleep holding each other.

※

In the morning, Peytra's hand glided along the silk sheets, reaching towards the body next to her. She was groggy from the night before and still blinded by the handkerchief, but aware of where she was. She felt for Jors and noted sadly that he wasn't there. Peytra called his name, but there was silence. She tentatively lifted the blindfold to see that the room she'd stumbled into was empty. The contrast between the way it had looked the night before and in the clear light of day could not have been more blatant.

The night before, the room had been foreboding, now in the streaming sunlight, it was open and joyful.

On the pillow next to her, she noticed a small letter:

Peytra,

Forgive me for leaving, but there is an errant task I must attend to. I will be back shortly to escort you through the passageways to your room. If you should wake before I return, I've left breakfast on the table.

Lovingly Yours,
Jors

There was indeed a large breakfast, which she only picked at. Then she noted a strange room off to the side with bathing bowls and tubs. She washed herself, dressed, and looked for a pen to write a short note.

Jors,

Don't worry, it's late, and I've gone to work.

Peytra agonized for a moment on how to return his sentiments in a way that was honest and still comfortable to her. She ended with:

Thank you for breakfast.

Affectionately Yours,
Peytra

With that, she snuck out of the room, hoping she wouldn't be seen. The hall was empty, and she walked briskly, looking behind herself when she crashed right into Kori.

"Well, morning!"

"Oh, yes, morning, Kori."

Kori peered behind Peytra to note that the Duke's door was slightly ajar. "Ah, so ya finally moved up here?"

"What?"

"Gani is going to be so mad I confirmed those rumors 'fore she did!"

"Wait? What? What rumors?" Then it dawned on her. "You KNEW?"

"It's a small castle, dear. Everyone knows. Have known for weeks. I mean, we all got a bit suspicious that His Grace was sending you letters alone, but then Cheri, you know Cheri, she's second head of laundry, and I just love when she sits with us because she smells like fresh soap, well, one night she saw His Grace sneaking out of your room a few weeks ago. And I like Cheri, but she told everyone, and since then, well, it's been a talk. We didn't really believe the whole thing either, or even if we did, we weren't about to judge. And Hue and Georgie were quick to squash any poor rumors in the guard. And, well, whenever anyone brought it up around Marcus, he put up a dramatic performance about how 'your love for one another was forbidden but eternal' and all that. And Gani absolutely forbid talk of those rumors in her kitchen and threatened to starve any person that dare murmured anything about it."

"Really?" Peytra could feel her face burning. All this time she'd been keeping this secret, or what she thought was a secret, and in truth, it'd been the talk of the castle. She was a strange combination of shocked, embarrassed, and angered.

"Yes, well, I mean, we did sort of suspect. And I thought it was a good thing. The Duke's not teeming with possible matches, and we like having you around. We just felt that if you wanted to say something, you would have."

"But why didn't you tell me that these rumors were going around? I... I would have wanted to know. Or that you believed them?" Peytra could feel a tear burning at the corner of her eye.

"There are rumors that circulate the castle all the time. You know that. And, well, this turned out to be true!" Kori blurted.

Before Kori could see her cry, Peytra turned and walked straight down the hallway to the small workshop to gather her tools. She didn't know what to feel, but right then, she settled on anger. On anger with the Duke for his carelessness. On anger with her friends for their gossip. But mostly on anger with herself, on some odd feeling of shame she felt about the secret of their relationship and how she'd become a target.

⚜

Peytra took out her anger on her final archway for the ballroom. Being enthralled in the manual work helped to physically relieve her frustration. She tried not to overthink everything but focus on the work. Cleaning up an edge here, a corner there. Adding the wax on top kept her moving, and her mind could take a step back from everything. It slowly began to dawn on her that her frustration was also tied to the precarious situation she was in. She was employed by the Duke, yes, but she was also his mistress. A position she didn't fully understand. Even the name to it felt foreign.

"Mistress," she whispered to herself for a moment as she took a small step back on the scaffolding to gander at her work. She spotted an area that was uneven when the light hit and searched for right tool. "Mistress." Peytra had ignored that portion of the whole experience, caring more for the odd pleasure the situation gave her. She enjoyed the Duke's attention and adoration. She enjoyed the sense of power it gave her, the sense of confidence she felt in the way he fawned over her. But how did she feel about him?

He was different for sure. In her little family's outcropping and in their village, there was never a man like him. Her life had been one surrounded by frivolous country boys, farmers, salesmen. Men she may have found attractive from time to time, but they went through life with such carelessness, without purpose. Peytra's focus on her work was a thorn, and thus, that attraction never lasted long. But the Duke's countenance was antithetical to that frivolity.

There was an area that could use more shading. She went to work on that and reflected on the first time she met him. His gaze was striking, if only for how steady and deliberate it was. How when he first held the little sheep toy in the shop, he was delicate with it. He treated it not like a toy, but a priceless urn or heirloom. But he wasn't always so serious. As she'd gotten to know him, she'd heard him laugh with abandon, and even though she'd never seen his face, she'd felt him smile. There were times where the Duke had a boyish charm. He had a tendency to envelop himself fully into things that brought him joy.

Whether it was the art she produced for him or herself. Even then his passion was deliberate, measured. But she enjoyed testing those limits, seeing if she could get him to unravel and get him to display some vulnerability.

At the end of all things, he was complex and contradictory. At once he was ominous and commanding in his position, and yet shrouded in his injury that he seemed so protective of. He could be oddly inquisitive but poised. He could be supremely gentle and affectionate, yet so distant in public.

Peytra paused to assess her work again. He was not unlike a good sculpture in a way. Sculptures and carvings were often full of contradiction in themselves. They were still and immovable but could evoke movement. The perspective was purposely exaggerated when carved, so that the onlooker could perceive it was correct. It was always the smallest details that took the most time to carve. But most often, the carver or sculptor, if they were in any way worth their salt, wasn't the one in control. They always let the wood, clay, or stone tell them what it wanted to be. Yes, Peytra could chip away at a block, she could pulverize it to make it work, but that work would be a violent aberration. If they worked with it, felt the way the material wanted to shape itself, the sculptor and the wood could make something truly incredible. They needed one another to make something greater than the sum of their parts.

There was a small bird song she could hear in the distance. She turned back to the door frame to take it in again. She thought for a bit about how, when all this was over, she would have to turn around and leave this work behind. That it would be here in this castle and the only thing to comfort her would be the memory of making it. Something seemed to drop in the pit of her chest at the thought of leaving. Whether it was because the Duke should marry or their contract end, it occurred to Peytra that she had grown to feel at home in this place, among its people. She had embedded little pieces of herself into the walls with her creations, and this evoked the feeling that on the inevitable day she would walk away tearing a part of herself in the process. But even more empty was the feeling that she would walk away from *him*, as he had left a part of himself carved into her.

Peytra had no reference for this situation or this feeling. There was the Marquis' mistress, but she'd never met them personally. And while the Marquis and his mistress seemed to be keen on taking the chance on love as it was, she wasn't sure she could. Nor was she sure that the Duke's love was strong enough to stay the temptation of a secure arrangement with someone else. The thought of him with the Baroness, for instance, infuriated her. Deeper than that, she wanted him to be happy, with or without her.

Was that love? Was it ultimately wanting someone else to experience joy so much at the expense of yourself? Even when there seemed no greater pain at the very thought of being without him, above her own self she wanted him to have some constant. There was a point where she couldn't distinguish between her sweat and her tears.

Hours later, while waxing the crevices of the frame, Peytra dryly realized she'd skipped her midday meal. Not that she cared to go to the kitchen at the moment, but her stomach heaved and begged a bit at its emptiness. Turning around, she had a small shock at seeing the Baroness, the Earl, Marcus, the Baroness' veiled attendants, and the Duke.

She'd been so engrossed in her work that she hadn't noted the little crowd that had gathered around behind her. They'd been watching her in fascination as she'd tied her sleeves to her shoulders and slowly pushed and rubbed the blocks of wax against the grain. Her hair had frizzed from the heat of her, taking up the better part of her figure. Her muscular arms moved rhythmically, pulsing but effortless. Her skin had become flush in the light and exhaustion, highlighting the brownness of her skin with a deep red. The Baroness, Marcus, and the Duke were keen to note the odd gracefulness of the sight.

It took a moment for Peytra to register that she had been watched. She hoped her eyes were no longer puffy from before. "Your Grace, Your Grace, My Lady, Marcus…" she said, bowing in turn. Her tangled locks fell about her face as she did so.

The Duke cleared his throat. "Peytra," he seemed to choke a bit, "we were taking a stroll and were curious of your progress."

Peytra felt something electric pass through her. She could hear the longing in his voice, and suddenly she felt that need as well.

"Yes, I was especially curious to see you work," said the Baroness, interrupting their stare. "What is it you're doing now?"

Peytra explained to the unusually rapt audience how she was finishing this section of archway. Such as sanding away the roughest edges, adding soot to the crevices to deepen the contrast, sealing the wood with a layer of wax, and such. Typically it was the work of an apprentice to do such things, but as

Peytra had none, she did this portion herself. She liked to work things to its final stages, so that if there were any mistakes, she could rectify as necessary.

"Jors! Why have you not gotten the poor girl an apprentice!" the Baroness squealed, playfully hitting the Duke. Peytra wanted to break her arm.

"Do you need one, Peytra? Would you like an apprentice? I'm sure we could arrange for one, should you like it?" the Duke said, with a guilt-filled fluster.

"No need, Your Grace!" Marcus had that distinctly mischievous smile on his face, "I will gladly offer myself up as her apprentice in all things physical, and of the heart!" He swaggered over and leaned against the scaffolding, "Simply instruct me, my dearest woodpecker, and I would gladly pound away at whatever tree you need me to, or wax whatever archway required. Let me be your student, love." Peytra couldn't help but laugh at his absurdity, but she had a feeling that the Duke was silently holding back an urge to throttle Marcus.

"I'd rather that you stay far away from my work, Marcus, less you break yourself, or worse, break something I've made," she teased back.

"Also, Peytra, before we forget our other purpose here, we wished to invite you to dinner tonight, that you may tell us more of your work and future projects," said the Baroness with a wandering gaze.

Peytra thought for a moment. The idea of eating with people she felt betrayed by at the staff's table seemed unbearable. She hadn't thought about how she would eat without somehow facing Gani or Kori or the others in the kitchen. "Yes, I would be delighted."

"Splendid, simply splendid," the Baroness said in a deep octave that had a sinister tenor to it. "What time is dinner again, Jors?"

"Seven, My Lady," intercepted Marcus.

"We look forward to seeing you at seven," said the Baroness with a smile.

※

Evening seemed to take forever to arrive. Peytra had finished the archway's entirety early and lay in her bed for an hour in hunger. She had motivated herself to get up and wash her face, then wrestled with her hair that, after a day's work unbraided and untouched, refused to be tamed. She heard a knock on the door and the softest whisper of her name. It was the Duke, there during daylight.

She opened the door and furtively pulled him into the room. The last thing she needed was more confirmation to the rumors she now knew existed. "Jors? Is there something wrong? What are you doing here? You could have been caught this early."

"Peytra, where is the blindfold?" He sounded breathless and commanding.

She looked about her and found it on the corner of her bed.

"Put it on," he commanded. He sounded forceful, and while Peytra remained wary and slightly frightened, she trusted Jors to know that he wasn't planning to hurt her. Something burned in the pit of her abdomen, and she acquiesced. She stood there, frozen and blinded, waiting for what was to come. "Jors? Answer me! Is something wrong? Has something happened?"

Within a moment, she heard the familiar rustle of his clothing being removed and he had wrapped his arms around her. He urgently kissed her ear and neck, moving his hands from her waist upwards. "Jors," she giggled, "we should get ready for dinner."

"The only thing I want to feast on is you," he said in between kissing her collarbone. In one movement, he lifted her up and placed her on her small bed. "I've been waiting to steal a moment with you. Your hair, your figure, it makes me beastly." With that, he began moving his hands up her legs beneath her skirt. Peytra melted and relaxed at his touch. He tucked his head beneath and started to untie her undergarments. She didn't protest but eagerly awaited his touch, excited for whatever surprise was in store. He seemed to breathe her in, and she instinctively felt his need.

His hands grasped at her thighs, and she noted curiously that his single hand could engulf her thigh. He kissed her along her legs, moving closer towards her center. Each one left her trembling with anticipation. When he finally reached between her legs, Peytra shook with such surprise she thought she would die and squealed with delight. Then he began to devour her in a way that she would have never imagined. He seemed eager to consume her, and Peytra was all too happy being consumed.

Then there was a loud knock on her door. Peytra stifled a moan and hoped that whoever it was would go away. Jors seemed unfazed or unable to hear and kept going. Pulling her close to him. The knock came a second time and much louder.

"Miss Peytra? Miss Peytra? We've been looking all over for you!" a woman's voice shouted through the door. It was faintly familiar to Peytra, and she desperately hoped whoever it was would go away, or else that she had her chisel so she could jam it down whoever's throat dared interrupt her.

Another set of knocks followed, this time loud enough that Jors paused to take note. Peytra was ready to murder the intruder. "That's Elle's lady-in-waiting," he whispered.

She shushed him. "Maybe they'll go away if we're quiet," she answered in hushed tones. She urgently wished him to continue.

"Better just see what she wants. I'll hide beneath the sheets while you get rid of her," he said, getting one last taste in for good measure before retreating under her blankets. When he was good and covered, she removed her blindfold and sorted her skirts. She knew she looked disheveled but frankly didn't care as she hobbled over to her door. She cracked it open. It was both of the Baroness's veiled attendants.

"Yes? Sorry, I was resting." Peytra tried to make it look as if she'd been awoken by their knocking.

"So sorry to disturb you, Miss, but our Lady has asked us to deliver something to you, and she had searched the entire castle." She gestured to her compatriot, who was holding a deep crimson swath of fabric. "Our Lady wishes for us to convey her regrets at the presumption, but she assumes that perhaps, due to your station, you may not have something appropriate to wear. She thus felt emboldened to loan you one of her very own fine gowns for the occasion. Our Lady wishes you to note that she picked this dress out of her own wardrobe with the hopes that it would be the most flattering to you. It has adjustable sides, back, and sleeves for a firm fit. And Our Lady is sure that the bold color will complement your lovely skin quite nicely. Our Lady hopes it shall be comfortable should you choose to wear it."

Peytra wanted to decline the dress at first, but then noted that the attendants would perhaps protest and delay her longer. Neither did she wish to insult the Lady or seem ungrateful, although she was cautious of the gift. She grabbed the mass of cloth from the silent attendant, trying to maneuver it to block her disheveled appearance. Peytra faltered for a moment. "Well, hmm, tell your Lady 'thank you' for such a generous loan."

As she was closing the door, the silent attendant stopped it with a surprisingly firm arm. The other continued, "Our Lady also instructed us to offer our services should you need it in dressing. That dress itself does require another person to tie the back appropriately, and while she would have preferred to be here herself to assist you in all your needs, she did not wish to impose too much on your privacy. But should you wish, we would gladly help you prepare for dinner. Atellia," she gestured to the silent attendant, "is also excellently skilled in hair design, and she works quickly, since the dinner is in half-an-hour's time."

"No, no, thank you, but no, I should be fine. Thank you, tell your lady thank you," Peytra said, this time truly rushing to close the door. It was then that she realized that a half-hour's time meant that she had to find someone to help her with the gown before heading there. She couldn't very well show up in one of her three dresses now that she'd agreed to this. Nor did she feel prepared to run and ask Gani nor Kori nor Una at the moment. She felt the material in her hands. It was a richly smooth, bright burgundy velvet. The smoothness of it reminded her of a clay her father had taught her to use, and the dye must have been the similar ochre and root for the dyes as her paints. There was small embroidery on the corners from what she could see. Ivy vines and fig leaves, as well as small jewels incorporated into the design. It may have been the finest piece of clothing Peytra had ever held in her hands, and she was supposed to wear it.

"Are they gone?" Jors asked, still hiding pitifully beneath the sheets. For the moment, her actual hunger, dinner, and the distraction had made her forget about the nobleman hiding like a scared cat in her sheets.

"Yes," she said with a faraway timbre to her voice. The pleasure she'd been eager to experience seemed to float from her mind as matters of the present flooded in. "Are we supposed to dress a certain way for dinner?"

"Well, the Earl and Elle will be there, as will the newer arrivals from this afternoon, the Viscount and Viscountess of Helbert, the Baron and Baroness of Pjerrin, and the Count of Martinny. It is customary to look presentable as such things."

"Then I've got half-an-hour to find someone to help me get into this dress, apparently." She was upset that she didn't know this, but more upset that no one had taken the courtesy to tell her this information.

"Peytra, I can help you. If you blindfold yourself, I'll help." He seemed to note her panic, and it suddenly dawned on him his oversight at not realizing that her life experiences were vastly different than his in these matters. He was pleading without saying so. She acquiesced.

The process of dressing became a surprising moment of intimacy. She stood there, blinded by the cloth as Jors gently untied the clothing she wore, patiently undressing her. He did take the opportunity to caress portions of her body, not in a lecherous way, but as a person admiring the body of their beloved. He wanted her, badly. But the propriety of the moment left him restrained.

Peytra relished the way he moved his fingers across her body. Her mind ran through a hundred excuses to skip dinner and for them to enjoy one another's company instead. It was her stomach that protested too loudly for it.

He gently helped her into the gown, tying and adjusting it to her comfort. He pinned and fit the sleeves, crafting it to her. It felt oddly familiar to do this, a task so mundane and reserved. When such things were finished, he also dressed, but left a firm kiss on the lips before sneaking back to his quarters to finish his own preparations.

It took her a moment to open her eyes and look downwards. Now that she was alone, she took the time to assess her image. The gown was a flattering cut, angled in such a way to order and enhance her body. The neckline seemed a little too low for her taste, and while in some ways her breasts now resembled the plumped shape of other noblewomen she saw, she felt exposed. There was even more detail than she'd noted before in the bordered embroidery that covered up through the ends of her pearl buttoned sleeves. She looked in her small table mirror. In the candlelight, the attendant was correct, the color of the gown enhanced the lovely brown of her skin. Even though she was more exposed than usual, it truly showed the lovely shape of her shoulders and collarbone.

Picking up her comb, she noted how stiff the gown felt in comparison to her other frocks. She had difficulty working her arms and hands through her hair to make a braided bun. *This must be what it's like to be noble,* she thought. *All this luxury, but it's hard to move. You can't dress by yourself or raise your arms. Couldn't sculpt or carve in this. It's tight, and I scarcely feel like I can breathe.* Though she had no real reason to, she suddenly felt for the Baroness.

It was five minutes too early when Peytra arrived in this finery, and she had to endure an awkward introduction to the Baron and Baroness of Pjerrin, and the Count of Martinny through their attendants. These nobles themselves seemed quite jovial and friendly, which was a relief. The Baron and Baroness were a particularly engaging couple, both with darker hair and eyes and roughly the same height. The Baron had the distinct mannerism of pausing right before he laughed with a booming bravado. The Baroness of Pjerrin was slightly more reserved, but also extremely sarcastic, which Peytra couldn't help but enjoy. She had a way of affirming something in a more serious tenor and then punctuating it later with a smile. As it was, the Baron and Baroness were a couple that fit well together, with an easy banter.

The Count was a much older gentleman. A widower with grown children off on "adventures" as he liked to refer to it. He had a grandfatherly sweetness about him. This did not mean that he wasn't prone to his own form of clumsy flirtation. He remarked adoringly that Peytra looked the very image of a Princess from the Southern Lands that he had met as a youth and wondered if perhaps she was that same Princess but having discovered the secret to eternal youth.

"No, no. I'm just the carver," she said.

"Oh, well, I was never so lucky as to have a carver as lovely as you," he said, bending a bit to add to his elderly effect.

"Don't let her beauty fool you, Count Allueishes, she's also quite talented," said a charming and melodic voice from behind.

"Oh, Elle! My dear," said the Count, straightening up and moving over to hug her warmly.

Peytra turned around to see the Baroness in a luscious green velvet and silk gown. The Count and the Baroness kissed one another on the cheek and began their small talk. The Baroness abruptly cut that short when she turned to Peytra and glided a step towards her.

"Peytra, my dear! Don't you look absolutely delicious." The Baroness clasped her hands to Peytra's in a familiar manner. "I knew that color would look lovely on you!" she beamed.

"Thank you, My Lady," Peytra bowed. "I truly appreciate your gracious, um, loan."

"It's nothing! You can repay me by finally letting me sketch you? Perhaps tomorrow during tea?" She reached out and gently tucked a stray hair from Peytra's head back behind her ear. Peytra was awkwardly struck by the overly familiar gesture. "Well? Would that be fine?"

"Yes," Peytra said, a little stunned, forgetting what she had agreed to.

They walked in and were seated at the table. The remaining dinner guests arrived. Peytra noticed that Una walked in and out of the dining area, as the Duke's right hand, she was often the formal head of the staff in manners like these. Peytra realized that she too must have been privy to the gossip surrounding herself, and she avoided Una's gaze, still too embarrassed that her secret had been poorly kept. For her part, Una seemed most preoccupied with seating the guests correctly that she seemed to avoid Peytra.

The Duke was the last to arrive in somber but more distinct finery. He would not be eating with them, as per his mask. It was generally believed that his appearance was so distasteful that seeing him eat would curb the appetite. But now Peytra resented that common assertion. She so desperately wanted to see him that she didn't care if people thought it distasteful. She wanted to eat and chat and look upon his face the way her mother and father did towards one another.

He looked toward her, seated close to the other end of the table on his right side. Even from there, she could see his eyes shift just a bit to note that he was smiling underneath.

The dinner itself was delicious. Whatever may be the case with Gani – talented for her age – she could prepare the fantastic from the mundane. Peytra indulged heavily on the meal as she hadn't eaten throughout the day. There was roasted pork and potatoes, salted fish filets, kidney pie, steamed evergreens, soup, and so on. Peytra dove into seconds to fill her emptied stomach. The Baron and Baroness of Pjerrin, the Count and Baroness of Retilk's lowlands, kept the conversation witty and apace. It was midway through that dinner that Peytra realized that these nobles weren't treating her differently or ,at least, were not constantly remarking on her lower status. While much of that could have been attributed to their particular temperaments, Peytra wondered if they also had knowledge of the affair and perhaps weren't eager to disparage someone close to the Duke. This needled her for the rest of the evening, souring her hefty appetite and causing her to avoid the Duke's indirect conversation and his direct gaze.

While the party decided to retire to the sitting room for drinks, Peytra bowed out of the festivities. That needled feeling had grown longer with the evening, and while she was entertained, she no longer wanted to linger on the discomforting thought that the kind nature with which they treated her was a charade. Walking back to her room, she found that a menagerie had camped out in front of her door.

Gani, Kori, Una, Hue, and Georgie, the people who had befriended her from the start, were seated on the floor, two open bottles between them, waiting for her. Peytra felt a warm little jolt in her heart for a moment, remembering the times they had gossiped late in the kitchens. Told stories to one another about their travels and the histories of this still strange place. While she now knew she was a part of that gossip, she came to realize that, in their own way, they all were. They were all a little part of the soon to be histories of the castle, and those histories would be documented in the talks of the kitchens and the whispers of the hallway.

The group paused for a moment and looked over and Peytra. Kori seemed ready to say something, but before Peytra could be undone by an awkward apology, she sat down on the floor in her ridiculous gown, grabbed the closest bottle, and took a swig.

"Well, that was interesting," she said with a smile.

They talked into the late evening, each bringing up their own opinion of the visitors. Each gave their own impression of the guests. Georgie, who had escorted the Earl on hunting trips, was able to best mimic his pompous attitude. He got up and raised his shoulders. "'Ah, you see that pheasant in the distance, I shot one exactly like that four years ago from 500 yards away. Why, the King once told me he'd give me a medal for my hunting prowess, would it not make the other nobility jealous.'" Georgie paused and smiled. "Not that the man could hit the side of this castle from more than three feet away. Kept blaming it on the gun, the air, and the 'relative humor of this region's atmosphere,' as he called it."

Una and Hue were a spitting image of the Baron and Baroness. They'd nailed their banter to an almost uncanny ability. Part of it, Peytra suspected, was because they aspired to be as well matched as the other pair was.

Meanwhile, Kori's impression of the Baroness's flirtatious attitude brought tears to Gani's eyes. The young head cook laughed so hard she fell over herself. Kori held onto her so she wouldn't hurt herself, and they laughed into each other's shoulders.

In time, the group remarked on the strange circumstances of Peytra's status and situation. For weeks Peytra had debated writing to her sisters for advice, but it didn't seem that they would be able to understand. And she feared one would crack and spill everything to their parents who would march up to the castle to pick out their daughter from the predatory clutches of the Duke. It was freeing for her to talk about her conflicted feelings with people who had more familiarity with ways these nobles operated. They didn't see "mistress" as a dirty word, especially when it seemed something born out of necessity. As Hue noted, there were many unhappily arranged marriages in upper classes. Una also added it was a frightfully common instance. She recalled her youth growing up in the holdings of a Baronet, who was cruel and condescending to his much younger bride. The lady took on a lover that stayed, even after the Baronet died.

Gani added her piece, that their king had made it clear to all the gentry that the only persons they could be given permission to marry were other titled people. When that was first known a few years ago, it echoed like a thunderous but mute clamp around the castle. There was a tacit understanding among the staff. That their deformed Duke, as kind as he was, could probably never find a bride if he couldn't offer them wealth or status.

"But here you are," said Kori. "The girl we didn't think could exist, who took on His Grace, and is someone he's in love with."

"Here I am," said Peytra. "I know what I am, a mistress. And I… I don't know what to do with that. I'm scared that he'll marry and have to dispose of me. I'm scared I'll have to leave when I've made this place home. And I…I like it here. I…" a few tears began to roll down her face despite her protest, "I love him." She smiled, resigned to herself that she had said it out loud. "I don't know why I do, but I do. I mean, I like it when we're alone. I can't see him, but I can see he's got a kind heart and a thoughtful mind. I love him, and I'm not even sure if he really loves me." Peytra wiped a few tears from her face while she tried to smile.

Kori took her hand. "Oh, he loves you. We all seen it."

"He does. He has it in his head to marry you, no matter the difficulty. I organize this place; he's got his eyes on you. Asked me to see about the costs of building a workshop here, and he's been at work with the King and other nobles to do something about that whole rule," said Una.

"And really, if you love each other, who cares if you're mistress or wife or something else. We know the truth, and we're here," said Georgie with a grand smile.

Peytra felt a warm candle flicker in her chest. She'd needed this type of friendship more than she could have estimated.

The next afternoon, Peytra was sitting as still as stone in the Baroness's room at the castle. It had a small, neat tea table and cushioned seats near an open set of windows. The light streamed down in steady, bright yellow diagonals. This room was on the western facing edge of the castle, and the sun could come in in the afternoon to light the room on fire.

Peytra was acutely aware of how much she was sweating. She felt one droplet form in the center of her temple. She could not move to wipe it away, as she was stuck being the Baroness's model for a sketch. At her request, Peytra had changed into a traditional frock that the Baroness had on hand. It was soft, breathable cotton and silk. And although it was far more comfortable and breathable than her normal wear, Peytra was over-heating. It was most likely due to the fact that she had never been in this position. The object of an artistic piece instead of the author. Now she was made to sit as still as her wooden carvings in an outfit that showed more skin than was typically appropriate.

For her part, the Baroness was diligent. Checking proportions against her thumb, moving her chalk with her gaze. Viewing both the page and Peytra at various angles as she drew. It was clear, from one artist to another, that the Baroness took this seriously and knew what she was doing. That thought didn't make Peytra any more comfortable, however. Instead she started to have an eerie *déjà vu* for all the times she'd made her friends and family pose for her work. It was better, she noted, to be the maker than the thing being made.

The entire situation seemed to be one made to put her in discomfort, and Peytra wondered if this was the Baroness's aim. It did not help that one of the Baroness's veiled attendants was playing a harp and the other reciting traditional poetry in an effort to keep Peytra entertained. This was also at the behest of the Baroness, who, having modeled for numerous portraits, stated she knew the importance of entertainment. Peytra noted that, while she enjoyed music, the few notes the attendant played repeatedly could scarcely be called such. And while she was never a fan of poetry, she was sure that the recitation of the other attendant would make her resent it. Peytra wasn't upset with the attendants as much as embarrassed for them. They seemed reluctant to partake in the entertainment as much as Peytra was reluctant to have to keep listening. But they all seemed to be slaves to the will of the noblewoman, even if they were more swayed by her charm than her status.

"There, I think." The Baroness pushed away from her board and tried to view the piece from a number of angles. "I tried my best to capture your essence as I could, not to mention the lovely shape of you. I have to say, I do think this is one of my better pieces, even if I didn't get your brow quite right, and couldn't really finesse the jawline as much as I'd like, I think... Well my dear, you were already a work of art."

With a quickness that belied the Baroness's insecurity, she flung her board around and showed Peytra. Staring back at her was a charcoal sketched reflection, but it also wasn't. Peytra had never felt as she did then, looking at this art that was her, but also wasn't. The sketch was uncanny and Peytra did not expect this level of skill coming from the Baroness. She had the curvature of her cheek, the fullness of her lips, the fullness of her nose to mirror-accuracy. But it also wasn't Peytra, the eyes were more intense, focused and powerful. The drawing's chin was more resolute, determined. The charcoal version of Peytra had a purpose, was not ambivalent of her wants or goals. No, this wasn't Peytra as she was, but as she desired to see herself.

Peytra stumbled to find the words. "My Lady, I..."

"Oh dear, you can call me 'Elle' here, I think we're past the point of honorifics if you've been in two of my gowns," the Baroness said with a sly smile. There was a muffled laugh from one of the attendants.

"Elle, I can't, I can't find the words. It's beautiful, I mean, it's me but more beautiful than I could be. And you are so skilled, I don't know what to say..." She gazed at the piece, mouth aghast.

In a smooth motion the Baroness sat next to Peytra and laid a feather-soft hand on her cheek. The Baroness smiled sweetly and looked deep into Peytra's eyes. "My dear, you are beautiful. And I fear my little drawing could only capture a fraction of that."

Peytra felt a nervous blush warm over her, starting in the middle of chest and reaching and burning her cheeks. Such that she couldn't help but blurt the fear that had been in the back of her mind. "Are you going to marry Jors?" At that Peytra wanted to bite the tongue out of her very own mouth.

The Baroness just chuckled a little. "Well," she said, tilting her face downward, "he is a dear friend and a good political match. And it is not like either of us are inundated with prospects. Why, he with his hidden body and I with my... um... reputation. Such a match would no doubt enrich both our regions and, as an understanding, we could both be with whomever we choose." At this she paused and took Peytra's hand with hers, onto the space between their laps. "I have of course, mentioned this to him at length. But it is of no matter to him. He has someone else, a certain gifted artist in his life that he plans on marrying, or at least being attached to singularly."

"He said that?" Peytra felt hope grow anew.

"He did but he didn't have to. Anyone could see it." The Baroness's mouth had a cat-like grin again. "Pity though," her eyes glanced downward and flickered up at Peytra, "we could have shared you."

The days that followed where a whirlwind throughout the castle, but Peytra was struck with an inner calm. The Baroness's confirmation that the Duke would not marry another nor send her away gave her the solid footing to make it through the castle in the throes of an invasion by various nobility. In the daytime she gingerly carved the Duke's new mask, giving each new draft an even more specific set of features. In the evening she would join the Duke and the ever-growing list of nobles at dinner. At night, in the dark, she would sneak and feel her way to the Duke's quarters, often to just enjoy his warmth and company.

If anyone was rattled, it was the Duke. His days consisted of settling petty disputes while trying to leverage and meet with the King. The King was becoming a consistent heel on his side; the man was intransigent, and the Duke was quickly losing patience for him. But losing patience could very well put him, or Peytra, now the known target of his affections, into a deadly situation. He would feel quite empty, lying awake at night, until Peytra would crawl into bed next to him. She was so tired she'd be asleep in the dark after her head hit the pillow. Jors would stroke her hair for a time and contemplate how to tell her.

But there was an agony to marrying someone who could be your undoing, and a terror in the knowledge that such a marriage would not be sanctioned. Jors only became resolute to his decision when he realized he could make her his heir in this way. That even if he were gone after these stolen moments of happiness, she would be taken care of. It was with those thoughts that he could sleep soundly beside her.

CHAPTER 12

Before either of them seemed to know it, the day of the ball arrived. Peytra registered it as Kori, Una, and Gani burst into Peytra's room in the afternoon as she was finishing the wax on the Duke's mask. They brought with them a rushed package from the tailor. It was the gown that had been commissioned for her and they wanted to watch her open it. She unwrapped the cloth and laid it out on the bed. It was nothing Peytra had ever seen anyone wear. The top was cut low in the South-easterly style, with a deep, black silk center insert. The majority of the gown was a bright, blood-red color, decorated with inset rubies and blackened embroidery. On the edges of both sleeves was an embroidered bird.

"Is that…" started Kori.

"Woodpecker," said Gani.

"Marcus," they all said in unison.

"I'm going to drive my chisel right through his eye…" said Peytra, flatly realizing what he'd done.

"Oh. Oh my." Una was floored. "I'll have the tailor make a new one. I'm so sorry Peytra. Maybe we can borrow a gown."

MASK OF THE NOBLEMAN

"No." The colors were bold; they were aggressive and they were the internal fire that Peytra instinctively knew she would need. "They want a woodpecker, they'll get one." She'd let herself be the portrait. She would be resolute.

Gani and Una had to leave to work on the final preparations. It was Kori who stayed and offered to help Peytra get dressed. She coiffed and braided Peytra's hair into something unique, high along the top. Kori left and came back, having absconded a haphazard collection of rouges, powders, and kohl. Kori did the favor of applying the foreign substances on Peytra's face. The kohl may have been too thick and the rogue a bit high, but Peytra looked into her small mirror and saw the determined face she needed to.

It was soothing for her to spend that time with Kori. They chatted as she primped and polished her up. And it was then that Kori finally felt comfortable enough to disclose the nature of her relationship with Gani. While applying the lip rouge, she couldn't help but say it, "I love her, I just do." Peytra knew that feeling all too well.

There was a light, secretive knock at the door. It was the Duke. Made up in the richly done dark hues, he seemed to be an even more commanding presence in person. Kori quickly excused herself but left a small kiss on Peytra's forehead for luck.

"Peytra, you look…" But before he could finish, she put a hand up to pause him.

"I know," she said with a smile.

"It's come to my attention that you may not have any jewelry to wear for the evening. Marcus was quite vocal on that and," his tone changed to one of annoyance, "he helped me select some heirloom pieces."

He'd been holding four wooden boxes with onyx

and ruby earrings, necklaces, and bracelets, each joined together by vibrant golds. He helped her put them on, and she noted how cold and heavy the weight of it all felt around her neck. Finally, he pulled out one final piece. A gold, filigree ring.

"It was my mother's," he said quietly, placing it on her finger. "Tonight, Peytra, I will be pulled in every direction. But I'll be there if you need me."

"Jors, likewise. I'll be there when you need me as well." She fingered the new ring. It was delicate but, like the other jewelry, came with a substantial amount of weight. He'd given her something precious, and now she would return the favor. She moved to the side of her bed, and lovingly wrapped in cloth was the mask she had labored over for him. She'd combined the face she had seen in her dreams with the features of his old one. He had given her so much in the short time they'd known one another. He'd introduced her to a new world and supported her skill. He'd given her a body unseen to the world. In return she would give him a face, one that reflected what she could see in him.

Jors unwrapped the cloth and was silent for a moment. Even though his true face was hidden, she could tell by the rhythm of his breath and by the way his eyes flickered that he too recognized the face. That it was a face which looked back to him in a mirror in solitude. "Thank you, Peytra. I don't think anyone could have given me this," he said, with a sadness that denoted his own shame in his reserve.

Peytra closed her eyes as he lifted his old mask to replace it with the new. When she opened them, she noted that Jors stood a bit taller. And while Peytra wasn't sure she'd ever see the face beneath, she found she could be satisfied with this for now.

"My love, it's time we were off," and he put his

arm out to escort her. She took it, and they left her room, unashamed of the scandal it could have caused.

❧

Peytra couldn't help but take a deep breath and close her eyes before entering the ballroom. There was still a crowd gathered near the entrance point, and she could hear the commotion from the doors. She suddenly felt her heart flutter, and her stomach turned over. Peytra hadn't expected that she would be this nervous. Jors gave her hand a reassuring squeeze before the doors opened.

It took her a moment for her eyes to adjust to the thousand lights. She'd spent much of her time in that great hall these past few months, carving those arches. But she'd been there in solitude, with the only sounds being her unconscious humming or the echo of her tools against the wood reverberating off the stone walls. Now the hall was filled with music and the ambient noise of a hundred little conversations. The arches she had agonized over for months now glowed in the torchlight, adorned with garlands of imported flowers. Cloth banners and standards brightened the room, turning the solemn beauty of the castle into a fantastical carnival. But what truly made the room were all the people in their ostentatious gowns and about all their masks. She'd forgotten that this would be a masquerade and her bare face was now a new source of anxiety. But she didn't have time to think before they were announced.

"Presenting His Grace, Jors Ameros the First, Duke of Palnero, Earl of Venteri, Viscount of Blading Hills, Viscount of Notreti, Baron of Sunning, and Lord of Fannery. And His Grace's guest, artist-in-residence, Peytra Sike," said the attendant. Everyone turned toward them as they walked forward, bowing in their wake. Jors said a few words welcoming the guests. This time they were not muffled by his mask because Peytra had carved the mouth in such a way as to increase the acoustics. Peytra could barely listen, however, as she was too busy trying to calm her breathing. They walked through and soon were crowded by various nobles. She couldn't help but hold on tightly until she heard a familiar voice behind her.

"Well, Peytra my dear, you clean up quite nicely. I'd go as far as to say that you look simply *delicious*." Turning around, Peytra was able to put the masked face to the voice of the Baroness, dressed in a deep sapphire gown and a matching bejeweled cat mask. Her two attendants stood behind her in matching grey dresses and mice masks.

"My Lady," Peytra smiled and bowed. It was comforting to be around someone she knew. "You look, well, like you should."

"Cheeky," replied the Baroness with a wink. "I do love masquerades. It's one of the few times you get to see who people really are." She pulled Peytra away from her tight grip on the Duke and began to escort her around the hall. She began to whisper into Peytra's shoulder like old, intimate friends. "Take a look around, and you'll see what I mean. Look to your left, in the sheep mask, that's the Barotney of Mintony. He has a propensity for following whoever has the influence of the King. As such, he's become a bit of a pariah at court, but you can count on him to go along with any popular suggestion."

The sheep-masked man was talking amongst a group of other such farm animals, loudly braying on about some occurrence. Peytra chuckled to herself.

"Or there," the Baroness continued, carefully pointing with her chin to a man with an elaborate sea creature mask. The mask had tentacle additions that went down his elaborately embroidered coat. He had black hair tied back from his face and a booming, operatic voice. "That's Count Beldlain," she said. "He's known for having his hands in everything. Financial investments, weapons, luxuries. And he has the very best gossip. As such, he's a dear friend." The Baroness waved to the count, and he smiled and nodded in return.

She continued to escort Peytra around. She seemed to seek out the more intriguing nobles as a chance to play on interesting observations. The Baroness turned her gaze on a woman a bit taller than the two, and Peytra's keen eyes noted how the Baroness's own eyes narrowed slightly. At first, Peytra thought that the look was predatory. She looked at the woman that had crossed their view — she was dark skinned, darker than Peytra, with black, curly hair that billowed out from behind her like a cloud. The noble had soft, delicate features, which contrasted with well with the deep, red-orange mask she wore. Noting the noblewoman's beauty, Peytra realized that the look the Baroness was giving her was not one of rivalry, but of curious attraction.

Really, she's no better than Marcus, Peytra thought and smiled to herself. "Who's that?" The Baroness seemed to suddenly register that she was not alone. "Oh, that is the Viscountess Dunawl. She's an old acquaintance."

"Why the fox mask then?" inquired Peytra, trying to playfully needle the Baroness.

"Well," she smiled deviously, "she is a vixen."

They continued to walk and talk around the hall like conspirators, and it occurred to Peytra just what was happening. She looked around to see that the other guests were also gawking at her and whispering among themselves. By keeping her in conversation, the Baroness was ensuring that Peytra was not a nervous wreck among the nobility. But it also served another purpose, Peytra deduced. Even with the Baroness's "scandal," she still retained a popular reputation. At least that much was clear to her in the way people flocked to her during the week. In many ways, the fact that she touted Peytra around the hall so fraternally was the public display of her approval of the carver.

But there was something else. In their afternoon talks, Peytra had learned that the Baroness had an almost magical ability to predict behavior and to determine what someone needed. It's what made her such a close friend to Jors and what was endearing her to Peytra. The trick now was to realize that the Baroness was teaching her, in a casual way, how to read the nobility.

They all wore masks, in one way or another. Peytra understood that easily enough. She'd worn the mask of her father's name for years. When people made comments about her lack of femininity, like Ottoh, she hid behind her wit and bit her tongue. Her face was a trained mask, and in many ways, she envied the nobles here tonight, who could express themselves beneath costume while not giving away their feelings. Yet, under those plaster coverings, they desperately wanted others to know them. By pointing this out, the Baroness was giving her a tool.

It occurred to her then that it may also be why Jors hid behind his. There was a comfort in not being seen. It worked to his advantage as a duke. Pushing aside his appearance, he was a deeply passionate and emotional person. Their months together and alone were proof. But due to his father's reputation, Jors was bound to passivity if only to keep the peace.

Then she thought about the bear. She thought about all the folktales with bears she had heard from her mother and others. A fearsome creature of great power, tempered by loneliness. In the stories, bears represented creatures loyal to their loved ones to a fault. In some cases they were emotional, frightening. By using the mask and making himself patient, kind, and wise, he'd taken his father's symbol and reclaimed it.

Peytra gave a gentle squeeze to the Baroness's hand and they looked one another in the eye. It was a silent thank you for the gift. A moment of understanding between friends.

They were interrupted by a stout burly man with a full beard and a badger mask.

"Peytra Sike, I presume?"

"Yes?" She tried her best to sound regal. "You are?"

"Unimportant, but Sir Xerves Rodham. The King requests you, Miss, for a private audience." The man was curt with an unreadable expression.

The Baroness gave Peytra a reassuring squeeze and then left her alone with the man as she waved to another friend. Peytra looked around her before following. The Duke was nowhere to be seen, and a pit seemed to open up at the base of her stomach. She'd come to understand some of the power these nobles wielded, but even they bowed to the King. Now she would have to present herself to a man 'whose guff reputation preceded him. Then there was the matter of what he'd want to speak to her about. Would he take issue with her as the acting mistress for a duke?

Would he forbid her from being with him because of it?

Walking down the familiar halls, Peytra's hands mindlessly fidgeted at her dress. She desperately wished she had a mask like the others to hide her growing anxiety. They stopped in front of the door, and Sir Rodham turned to look her other. He picked off a stray string that danced on her shoulder and brushed her shoulders off. "When you go inside, do not look him in the eye until addressed. Refer to him as 'Your Highness' and make sure to keep your chin high. He hates fear."

The look she gave must have conveyed the silent question as to why he'd given his advice. He looked at her, then back to his hand on the doorknob. "Ten years ago, the Duke gave a small loan to a blacksmith's apprentice to begin a path to knighthood. He's never asked for it back. I will forever be grateful."

In a smooth motion he opened the door, straightened his stance, and beckoned her into the room. Keeping her eyes mostly to the floor, she immediately recognized the large mahogany table. The King had set up court in the Duke's meeting room. She bowed as low as she could, stating, "Your Highness." She stayed until the King addressed her and allowed to her rise. Now she looked directly in front of her to a man casually seated in one of the plush chairs. He was much plainer than she'd imagined and of average height. He had reddish-brown hair and slightly crooked nose, with the rest of him swallowed by elaborate gold robes. A rich, gold lion mask was casually placed on the table next to him.

For her moment, the nervousness that had clouded her abated. After all, this was just a man. A king, but not a god. Still a man, and a man could be reasoned with, or so she thought. But then she glanced over to the left, and sitting at straight attention was Jors. Covered from head to toe, he could have been mistaken for a statue, calm but severe. Yet Peytra had come to know him better. Knew by the slight curvature of his spine, the rigidity of his shoulders, that he was angry or nervous or both.

There were a few guards and attendants, but this little gathering was such a cold contrast to the revelry just a few halls away. For a moment, everyone seemed to melt away, and it was just her, the Duke, and the King.

The latter shifted his gaze to the Duke. "This is her, Jors?" Peytra could already measure his disdain by his tone.

"Yes," the Duke replied, with what was obviously forced calm. "This is Peytra Sike. My sculptor and betrothed."

She looked forward again, registering the mask more finely. What would the Baroness say about a man such as the King in this moment? He picked a lion, so he wished to communicate power and majesty. The obscene garishness of his outfit was clearly meant to let everyone know of his wealth. The casual way in which he spread himself across the chair, as if he was a bored and discontent youth, was clearly meant to show his own personal disdain for them. In short, he was grasping at power like only a man afraid to lose it would. He did not have the natural grasp for power the way that Jors did, who even as a boy inspired loyalty of his household. He didn't have the quiet, fierce leadership inherent in Gani. He did not naturally come to power, so instead he dressed in it. He was playing a part.

Thus, when he tried to demean her it was meant to be a game. A game that Peytra was going to play –

and win. She stood a bit taller, slowly threw back her shoulder, lifted her chin to meet his gaze. She would challenge him – a bird against a lion.

The King met her gaze for a flickering moment and then looked over to the Duke. "Well, she doesn't look noble-born." He looked back to her. "Well, Miss Sike, was it? What can you tell me about your heritage? Do you have some mysterious royal lineage I nor Jors are aware of?"

Peytra kept her look cool and measured. "Not that I am aware of.. My father is a well-known master carver and toymaker who taught me my trade."

"And what 'trade' is this?" The King snickered at himself, and Peytra could hear Jors take in a breath in anger.

Instead of getting angry, she felt something in the pit of her stomach take shape. It pulled and tugged at her, guiding her to the words she needed to say. "My trade, Your Highness, is carver. Even if I had noble blood, I'd scarcely look it. My hands are calloused and rough from the work." She took a moment to look derisively at the King's delicate hands. "My arms lack the slender grace of a noblewoman's. And anywhere I look, I see the patterns I could make from raw wood or plaster. I may not be royalty but mine is a noble profession."

"And so you wish to marry a duke then? To soften your hands and be pampered?" the King bit back, now sitting up.

"No," and Jors turned his head in shock, his eyes asking her for a reason behind the betrayal. "I don't want to marry a duke, Your Highness, I want to marry Jors. And I would marry him if he were a stable boy, a farmer, and, yes, even a duke. Nor do I plan on softening my hands. My very nature is centered on what I create, on how I shape the world around me. It was the thing that Jors first saw in me. I didn't charm him with my pedigree, my lands, my wealth. It was my ability that drew us together and it is a part of me I will not deny."

Peytra was now shaking beneath her dress, but was determined to keep her face and hands as still as marble. She'd just raised her voice to a man who had the power to kill her and her entire family without consequence. Even now, she had a dreadful chill down her spine at the thought of her mother being dragged, kicking and screaming, out of their home by brutish soldiers.

The King's eyes narrowed for a moment, hawkish and predatory. "Jors," he said after a moment, not removing his gaze from her, "what an odd specimen you've brought before me. I'm not quite sure why you'd wish to wed such a thing, who would not be a *suitable* person for the title."

Something seemed to hum in the room then, a current emanating for the Duke. Peytra took it as an illusion of the stress, but she noted how the King shifted in his seat. Somehow the Duke had made his anger palatable.

"You will not speak that way to my betrothed, *Your Highness,*" Jors growled.

The King was visibly cowed but attempted to hide it by straightening his spine. "You forget your place, *Jors*. As my subject I am free to speak to her as I wish."

"And you forget, Your Highness, that your power is only as good as the nobles who behold it," Jors bit back. It may have been an illusion of the light, but Peytra could have sworn that he had grown taller.

The King leaned forward to give Jors an incredulous sneer. "What, precisely, are you saying, Jors?"

"He's saying," Peytra interrupted, suddenly needing to calm them before regicide became an option, "that outlawing the marriage of the classes, it's — it's preventing all of them from continuing their lines." Something began to run across her memory, it was a conversation with Marcus and the others about the dangers this practice would do to the stability to the kingdom. She let the words form themselves in her mind before continuing. "The more you prevent this, the more you sew unrest and resentment among the nobility. Not only that, you prevent the nobility from bearing heirs. And that'll just lead to disputes when they pass. A duke with no heirs can easily be the start."

"Then let the nobles marry one another," the King said.

"Many do. But even while so many marry for love or the advantages those matches come with, you cannot force people to marry or bear heirs. A poor, forced match would hardly gain your loyalty. There will always be people in love, as I love Jors. Preventing that union does no favors to your rule."

"Ah, yes, and sustaining every little harlot social climber is going to do well for the crown." The King let go a sardonic laugh. "My father degraded the family lines like this, allowing every sired maid's bastard a chance at a title, and I've been contending with it."

It was a bolt of lightning that struck her. That was it. There had been the whispers of another contender to the throne, and he'd given her the fodder to use it. His father had sired a son with a commoner, and now this son had a chance to usurp if enough dissatisfaction crept through the kingdom. But it was more than that.

She thought of how she would carve him. It

would be him, seated on an ornate throne and his figure leaning forward, uncomfortable with the position. She would keep the wood raw and unfinished, as he was. He didn't know what kind of king he wanted to be, and he was clouded by that insecurity. The angles would be jagged and pointed, and there would be that look in his eye, somewhere between a petulant son fighting with the necessity of the office. For a moment, she saw him as he was, as someone in a position they needed to possess but did not want. For a moment, she felt a small pain for him, for despite his cruelty, it was a poor costume for what could be. She needed to grasp onto his sense of duty. She would help it bloom.

"Your Highness," her voice lowered to a soft and kind whisper, "I do not know what could make you think of your citizens so." She looked him in the eyes. "I grew up the daughter of a toymaker, I have been surrounded by every shade of commoner. The farmer who grows the oats for feed, the schoolteacher who gives children the power to read, the carpenter and the merchant. We are the blood of your kingdom, each day rising to live in our pursuits. Each day making this kingdom the peaceful success it is. Please do not paint every commoner as lowly or less."

The King weighed her words for a moment. Jors stood gazing at her, his eyes unreadable. The King smirked then. "Well, perhaps I may have been wrong about you Peytra. But let me ask you this. Would you still marry a duke if you had the opportunity to instead be with a king?" He leaned back in the seat, feigning confidence.

Peytra and Jors were both dumbstruck by the proposal. Jors paused, unable to fully comprehend what the King had just said. Peytra blinked for a moment and then regained her composure, she replied smiling, "I am flattered ,Your Highness, but I love Jors, and that is who I wish to be with."

Half his lip lifted into a smirk, something shifting in his eyes. "Pity. Well, then. I believe this conversation has run its course. You may await my decision." And he waved them off, dismissing them into the hall.

The pair blinked at one another.

"How do you think it went?" Peytra asked.

Jors placed his gloved hand on the side of her face. "I'm not sure. He's quite... mercurial. I know you were splendid while I very well was close to treason."

Peytra smiled when an idea struck. "Jors, do you know how to get to my workshop from here?"

"Of course."

"Then lead me there."

They reached her small workroom which was still cluttered with wood shavings, sketches, and tools. On a side table was a small carved peony she'd used as a practice for a larger work. She picked it up, cradling the delicately worked carving in her palms. Using the castle's numerous tunnels, Jors lead Peytra back to the substitute throne room. Saying a small prayer to Fregh, she entered the room uninvited. The King was still seated, dictating something to an assistant when she burst in to confront him. It was clear that he felt his quipped proposal had unmasked Peytra for what she was. Instead, before he could say so, she opened her palm to present the carving.

"Your Highness, here is a token of my work. Of what commoner's hands can make. May we all build a better kingdom tomorrow," she said and quickly turned away before he could reply. She was so quick that she didn't note how the King held the piece in his hands with the tenderness of holding a real flower. He looked to the impossibly thin petals which glowed in the candlelight and a smile uncontrollably crawled across his lips.

Before returning to the crowds, Jors and Peytra decided to abscond to the side garden to catch their breath. They were silent for a while as they strolled the small, fall-lit path in the moonlight, her arm interlinked with his. In the distance they could hear a night bird calling out into the star-speckled darkness.

Jors turned to Peytra. "Are you cold?" he said. The steam of his breath floated between the slats of his mask into the chill air.

She smiled and shook her head. "No. Well, yes, but it's nice. It's good to feel the cold on my skin. Besides, I don't know what Marcus had this made out of, but I'm hotter than a furnace."

Jors chuckled. "Well, I hope you don't mind, but some of that velvet you won in the spring festival was used for the dress. The red however, I believe it's a type of wool from the North province. It's the only place that makes that particular shade. Marcus went on and on about it when he showed me the design he'd drawn up."

"You *knew*!" Peytra exclaimed and gave him a playful shove.

"Of course I knew. You didn't care or want to be involved, and Marcus was all too happy to flaunt this whole thing in front of me. Besides, you look wonderful in red. I couldn't turn down the idea."

"Yes, but a woodpecker?"

"They are clever, industrious creatures. Would anything else have suited you?"

Peytra smiled to herself. She was no disdainful cat or elegant swan. She was what she was and happy to be it. As the air chilled, her expression turned somber. "Why me?"

"What do you mean?"

She paused in her step. "I mean, you're a duke, with a lot of money and a lot of power. Even staying hidden, there must have been… others. People who you could have courted? People who you wouldn't have to go through so much to be with?"

He stopped and turned to look at her, measuring his words. "I know what people must think of me. What they must think of my body with all the stories that circulate. What they must see when they look at me. And this… situation has rarely been conducive to close relationships or courtships because of it." He paused to look up at the moon, glowing a clear white at this hour. "I inherited my position at much too young an age, and I was lucky that, despite my condition, I was surrounded by good and loyal people who raised me well."

His stray hand reached out to touch a nearby bush. "The situation of my position means that I meet young women who would be suitable wives to a man in my position. They were trained from a young age to smile and be kind to any suitor, no matter how old or hideous or distasteful they may find them. My presentation would shock them for a brief second and then they would smile. I do not blame them for their necessary false smiles, and in truth, this has resulted in good friendships, but not love. I was resigned to never find such a person. And then, do you remember the first time we met?"

"Yes. In my father's town shop."

"Yes, it was warm and I was unnerved at this new attention by the massive crowds. I was in no mood to be introduced to a shopkeeper and his relative as I saw it. The first time you saw me, you looked uncomfortable for the briefest second, yes, but then I saw something else. You kept looking at me, you kept trying to see me. Then I looked back at your face, which was so pretty and new. And then I saw your sculpture, and I fell in love with that deft hand. That such a hand belonged to you is one of the greatest blessings of my life. I am in awe of your talent, that you make things with your skill and a few raw materials. That you create and bring new into the world is wonderful. But then that you are kind and clever and funny is almost too good to be. I'm not a poet, Peytra, but you're beautiful in ways I could not have conceived. Every part of you is a dream to me."

Peytra flushed at all this praise, the smile moving into her chest. She felt lightheaded and leaned into Jors. Looking up at him doe-eyed "Do we need to go back to the party?" And he just laughed.

By the time the pair had reached the Banquet hall once again, the ball had descended into a raucous affair that knew no boundaries, including those of class or rank. Cask after cask of aged wines and liqueurs had been opened and drunk dry. Maids danced with guards and baronets alike. Guards, stable hands, and other residents flirted and courted countesses. They were dancing, eating, drinking, singing bawdy songs, and engaging in all manner of frivolity. Masks were half worn and half covered reddened faces. The band had evolved into a conglomerate of painstakingly trained musicians and their countryside counterparts. Violins strung notes along with fiddles, matching ever faster rhythms in an unspoken challenge. Silver flutes competed for high notes with wooden ones while deerskin drums were brought out and beat along.

Peytra and Jors looked at one another in the silent understanding of parents watching their charges amuse themselves. By the twinkle in his eyes, Peytra knew that he was smiling beneath the mask. They were approached by two of the loudest revelers, Marcus and the Baroness, both of whom were disheveled and reeking of wine but with grand smiles on their faces.

"Well, I suppose I have at least one of you to blame for my court being such a mess," Jors said with enough humor so that anyone could take his meaning.

Marcus laughed and clapped Jors on the shoulder. "We just wanted to make sure you had a memorable party to celebrate your engagement!"

"Engagement?" both said in unison.

"Yes! Jors, you dog!" the Baroness squealed. "The King Himself came in and made a big announcement congratulating you two and the Viscount!"

Peytra was ready to faint and grabbed hard onto Jor's hand.

Marcus noted her paleness. "He did! It sent this party into a frenzy! Congratulations!" And he took Peytra's face into his hands and kissed both of her cheeks, then proceeded to do the same to an equally stupefied by joyous Jors.

That action set off the rest of the party to give their congratulations one by one. The nobles, the staff, their families, came forth with hugs and handshakes. Even the lightly intoxicated King.

However, there was one mysterious guest that avoided the pair. Peytra spotted the long red hair in the distance and the white of an unmistakable swan mask that hid in the shadows of the vast ballroom. She seemed eerily familiar to Peytra, but as soon as she blinked, the mysterious woman vanished, and Peytra took it as a trick of the light and the night's excitement.

Though it was not thought possible, the band struck up even louder and faster than before. Jors offered his hand, and the clumsy pair made their way to dance. Or, at least, something akin to dance as neither had managed a lesson. Instead, they fell onto each other laughing as the room joined. It truly was an event that would be talked about and reminisced for years after, provided they could all remember it.

Peytra woke up late in the morning. She removed the blindfold and looked down. She remembered how she'd (loudly) asked Jors to go to bed late in the Ball. Her drunken exclamation would be the gossip of the season. Recalling that, she had to laugh. She remembered getting undressed and crawling into bed, and that she tried to tie the blindfold but her drunken fingers could not manage. She remembered how his warm body hugged her in the night, and that they had gone to sleep speaking of wedding plans.

Lying next to her was a single, sweet-smelling primrose. She smiled when she put it up to her face.

CHAPTER 13

The following month found Peytra in the middle of a storm of tradesmen and vendors, trying to make decisions about her wedding. This was all new to a girl who'd only witnessed a handful of weddings that were mainly village affairs. She remembered her brother's and sister's weddings, when the family did everything, the cooking and dressmaking. The sprucing of the house that always ended up her task. Yes, it was hectic, but when she reminisced over the lengthy chats while mending dresses or how her brothers would pick her up to hang garlands, she felt a warm feeling wash over her.

This wedding planning was nothing like that. While both she and Jors wanted a small, private, temple affair, which would be fine, there needed to be a grand banquet to accompany it due to Jors' station. As soon as the announcement rang out, Peytra was immediately hounded at all hours by a parade of merchants. They came while she was carving or eating lunch. Once, while on a solitary walk with Jors on the grounds, a tailor jumped out of the bushes and accosted her with samples.

Her typical recourse was to run and hide. Barring that, she would send them to Una, who quickly noted to Peytra that these were not her decisions to make. It was best if they found her in the kitchen because Gani had no issue running them away with a rolling pin or butcher knife in her hands. But since she couldn't take Gani with her wherever she went, Peytra was forced to try ever more creative excuses.

"I don't know why they don't just go to you?" she said one evening by the fire in Jors' study.

"I have no issue dealing with them, but I think in many of the over noble households, it tends to be the mother or the wife who are given these planning responsibilities. I have to think that they've become accustomed to seeking them out," he said, peering over the text he was studying.

Peytra took a deep breath. "Well, they shouldn't be so...bothersome!"

"No, they should not." He paused. "I think there may be a degree of pressure for them. Noble weddings are few and far between, and that sort of business, should they impress some, can lead to continued, steady, high-paying work. It doesn't excuse the behavior, but I suppose I can understand it."

Peytra recalled how Ottoh had also been determined to gain a duke's favor and let out a heavy sigh, "I know. I understand it too, I just would like quiet. This is too much. At least the others are helping when they can. Even Marcus has a job."

"Oh?"

"Yes, he's to design and commission my wedding dress. He insisted. I told him that if he pulls the same stunt as he did for your birthday that the next thing I would be chiseling would be his face."

Jors let out a deep laugh. "Well, that's my love."

"What are you reading?"

"Oh, this? It's a categorization of stories relating to the Polodians. This translation is in Galarian. It just came in today."

She lifted an eyebrow in cautious curiosity. "Ah, still working on that problem?"

"Yes."

"Any, um, progress?"

Jors was silent and looked at the fire. "Not as of yet...but I'm hopeful."

Curiosity itched at her like a rash until finally, "Jors, what is that problem you're trying to solve?"

"Peytra, I..." He held something back as his breath caught in his chest. "I can't tell you. Not just yet." He shook his head and then closed the text. Changing his tone, he stood up and took her hand and said, "Let's go to bed."

As they walked out of the study, Peytra peered behind her at the book laid haphazardly on the side table. He'd become more and more concerned with getting these texts in the last month. She couldn't help but notice the increased stack in his quarters or how he was spending more and more of his spare time pouring over the works. As they were in multiple old tongues, she could never decipher the titles. She knew he was educated, but never knew that he could read Galarian, Rhodarian, Dexturian, or Iktash. Peytra always got the feeling that she was violating something deeply personal whenever she asked about it.

Instead, she'd sworn Marcus to secrecy and was having him teach her some of the languages between breaks. She'd had four weeks of Rhodarian and could still only translate rudimentary sentences in the ancient language. It isn't that she wanted to violate his privacy, she just wanted to connect with him. More than that, she wished to solve whatever issue seemed to be eating at him. His demeanor hadn't changed since their engagement, but there was an ache that sat in their moments of silence. She felt it when he reached for her at night, burying his face in her hair. She felt it on their evening walks as he stared at the sunset. No matter how much they'd grown to love one another, it was a tentative bridge across the chasms between them.

That book was a reminder of the secrets Jors was keeping. Secrets of his problem. Secrets about his body and face beneath the mask. Peytra resisted the urge to throw it into the fire.

One very good thing that had come from their engagement was that Peytra had been moved to quarters adjoining the Duke's. These were the apartments traditionally given to the lady of the house. They'd been remodeled when the Lady Swan had been here. It had been boarded up and the furniture covered in large tarps after her death. The castle staff took a full two-days cleaning and repairing the room before surprising Peytra with the gift. She'd cried and felt foreign in the grand splendor of it.

Looking at the candlelit rooms, she still wasn't fully accustomed to it. Whereas the Duke's quarters were dark and somber – something left over from his father's frightening disposition –the Lady's quarters were meant to be a distinctive contrast. Even at night, the starlight that streamed in from the high windows reflected off the mural in the ceiling. It depicted the birth of the universe, when the great nothing dreamt of light. The bands of that light headed into every direction. Peytra noted, with a professional eye, that the artists had mixed mica into the paints so that the art glittered. At the very tip of every ray was an iridescent crystal point, which glowed in the starlight.

The walls throughout the apartments were also adorned with murals. They were all nature scenes of great beautiful beasts frolicking in springtime. True to form, there were numerous swans, lazily swimming on a distant pond. These murals had been touched up before she moved into the apartments, and her heart swelled when she saw the woodpeckers that now adorned the trees of the murals. By the vibrancy of the paint, she knew these were recent additions. She choked back her tears at their acceptance of her.

The most startling thing was the massive, white-marbled fireplace. It was attached to the wall that bordered Jor's rooms. They were separate fireplaces that met in a single flue. She liked to imagine their fires meeting and intertwined like lovers as she ran her hands over the ornate sculpture. It depicted the apocryphal tale of Eliath and Cressida. Two lovers who were set to meet in a different land. Eliath's boat was lost at sea, and he was marooned on an island for three years. Cressida's ship had been captured by pirates, and she'd been enslaved in a different land. When both escaped their situation, each thought the other had passed.

Neither Eliath nor Cressida could live without the other, so they took to the great mountain Ikti to try to climb to the heavens to ask the gods to bring their lover back. When Cressida reached the top, Fregh just smiled and entertained her for ten days until Eliath reached the top. When they grew old and died in one another's arms, the gods immortalized their souls into the pair of southern stars known as the Campi.

So the fireplace showed their shipwrecks on either side of the hearth. It transitioned upwards to two small figures climbing upwards, turning the chimney into Ikti. At the top, they embraced. Looking at the ceiling above the fireplace, Peytra could make out two crystal stars.

There was the giant bed, which for Peytra was a dream. It had white lacquered posts that wove together like branches, and a beaded canopy that looked like the night sky. Sometimes Peytra would lie there in the afternoon and try to make out the constellations. If Jor's joined her, then he would recount the tales behind each star in candlelight. Sometimes she would listen to him excitedly recount some figure and close her eyes. She'd imagine he was not wearing that mask that was starting to weigh on her. No, she thought of the man she dreamed he might be under there. Sometimes he had scar tissue, sometimes not. She loved both, but as her wedding approached, she grew more and more alarmed that she was going to be marrying a man she had never seen.

Peytra trusted Jors with her life, but her heart had a tender spot of ever-growing anxiety. That fear was only mildly soothed by all that he shared with her in every other context. She thought about that discomfort as she disrobed in her bathing area. She washed her face and absentmindedly walked to what was once a private office space, but had been converted to a small workspace. Sketches now littered the elaborately carved desk. Unlike her workspace in the other area of the castle, wood scraps did not litter the floor. As the soon-to-be lady of the castle, Una had let her know that she was to have a lady's maid. They'd hired a local village girl named Gia to the task, and it unnerved Peytra to no end to have someone cleaning up after her. She endeavored to never do any messy work in her apartments. One time she'd brought in a small model she'd wanted to alter. When she returned from a walk that evening, the desk was spotless, and it guilted Peytra to no end that this young girl had to clean up after her. From then on, Peytra took care to clean her rooms as much as possible in order to spare Gia. Inevitably she would miss something, and the apartment would be even more spotless than before, and this was a source of constant consternation.

After organizing her projects for the next morning, Peytra walked to the wall that connected her apartments with Jors' and to the hidden slot that ran through it. She'd heard competing stories as to why that slot existed. According to Kori, the slot was there in case the Duke or Duchess was ill, they could still communicate with one another. According to Jors, it was because his great-grandparents had married to unite their territories, but absolutely despised one another, so this was the only way they communicated.

Perhaps neither story was true, or perhaps some combination of the two or more. Either case, Jors and Peytra utilized it in a wholly different way. They sent small love notes to one another throughout the day. On his end, Jors would sometimes copy old poems into small pieces of parchment, or he wrote little missives about the things he loved about her. If he was particularly inspired, the notes were reminders of what he planned to do with her. Those notes often gave her a deep blush and made her toes curl.

In her replies, Peytra had resorted to sketches. She'd not had the education Jors had, and words were never her strong suit. Instead, she sent him doodled notes that she sometimes captioned. She drew little images of bears and woodpeckers, of sculpture ideas, or comedic cartoons. If she was feeling particularly adventurous, she would disrobe and sketch her body in different positions. She always felt a little tingle of excitement when she put those sketches into the slot.

There was one sketch that she was too afraid to send. It was a picture of the face she saw in her dreams. She desperately wanted some confirmation that that was Jors. But even more deeply, she feared that she would hurt him by showing him a face that held no scars.

Opening the false plate, she called to Jors and asked if he was ready for bed. That was their nighttime routine now. Calling to one another through their secret compartment in the wall and deciding in whose quarters they wished to sleep. Peytra thought about those books piled in his apartments and invited him to her quarters. She wanted to keep her mind off the question he was searching for. Jors took down the candles in his rooms and made his way through the hidden passage that connected their two living spaces.

For a time, they lay in in her bed, he fully clothed while she was just in her shift. They talked with the conversation shifting easily from the familiar to the untread. They started with their favorite childhood memories. For Jors, he remembered the first time he rode a horse on his own. He talked about the freedom of running across a field at breakneck speeds. There was the pressure of the wind as it pushed back against his chest when he was fast upon a steed that knocked the wind from him. The freedom that pressure symbolized was a delight for him.

Peytra talked about how her brother Peytire saw her first carving of a cat and told her it looked like a hobbled gopher more than a cat. She told Jors about how she'd thrown her little carving at Peytire so hard it left a small scar under his eyebrow. They laughed, Jors' laugh coming deep within his chest.

"Well, he wasn't wrong," said Peytra after a bit. "It looked like some drowned creature. But my wee hands were just starting."

He chuckled once more and then turned to her slightly. He ran his gloved hand through her hair. She could see his blue eyes documenting her appearance, and she resisted the urge to take up her hands and pull off the mask. "I have a question."

"Yes?" She tried to stifle a murmur as his fingers lightly massaged her scalp.

"What was your first kiss like?"

Peytra had the vague feeling a deer must have while being hunted. "Well, hmm, let me think for a moment."

"I'm just curious," he said with sincerity.

"Hmm. When I was seven, I kissed Ottoh's visiting nephew. He had a sweet I wanted, and he told me he wouldn't share. I offered to kiss him for it. He said girls were disgusting. Then, naturally, I threatened to kiss the little toad. He just stuck his tongue out at me. I grabbed him by the shoulders and planted my lips on his. He ran off screaming and threw his sweet in the mud."

Jors laughed for a good minute until Peytra playfully elbowed him in his ribs. "Truly, what was it?"

"Who was yours?"

He lay back. "Elle."

"Really?" Peytra propped herself on her side, part of her slip sliding off her shoulder in the motion. Jors was noticeably distracted by the movement before he answered.

"Yes. Well. Neither of us had ever kissed anyone. I was still young and new to being a duke. It was more out of curiosity than anything else. She wanted to, as a point of exploration for her, and thought she could do so with me."

"Did you make her wear a blindfold?"

"We didn't have one on-hand. So I covered her eyes with my hands. I supposed I was a bit crestfallen when she said that the kiss confirmed her suspicions."

"Oh? What suspicions were those?" She settled herself in the crook of his shoulder.

"That she preferred women," he nursed a chuckle. "Now, no more stalling. Your first real kiss."

"It was in Summer, after some sort of village affair. His name was Carl. I'd been in that sort of girlhood love with him since I was a child."

"How old were you?"

"Thirteen, I think. And Carl is a neighbor from a farm. He's married now with a brand new son."

"And?" Jors pressed. Peytra pursed her lips for a moment.

"And I used to be enamored with him from afar. He was just a bit older than me, but he seemed much older. More adult. And so, one day during the Spring Festival, I gave him a slice of my mother's dated pie and asked him to dance. And then I kissed him. And he was kind. But he did not feel for me the way I felt for him. But that was youth."

"Peytra," Jors said gently, stroking her face. Unknown to her, a tear had welled in the corner of her eye. She wasn't sure what made her so sad. Perhaps it was the memory of rejection. More likely, it was the remembrance of a youth that had come to an end far too soon.

Jors did not pester or prod. When the tear escaped her eye, he gently brushed it away and pulled her into him. Feeling safe and warm, she let the tears of distress flow freely to soak his clothing. He rubbed her head and back and whispered all the ways he loved her late into the night. She didn't notice when she fell asleep, drained of her worries, in his arms.

※

The snow had just begun to fall when Georgie pounded his fists against Peytra's door. She looked up from the mound of papers that had buried her under her desk with a sudden alarm. The pounding continued as she ran to the door and was greeted by an out-of-breath Georgie, who was doubled over, snow still clinging to his black hair.

"Georgie? What's wrong? Is Jors ok?" All her fear poured into her, and every little suspicion crept under her skin.

He stood up, a large grin plastered on his face. "Nothing's wrong. You have visitors."

"Visitors?"

"Yes, your brother and sister."

Peytra covered her face for a moment and took a deep breath in frustration. "Georgie! I thought something had happened! Why'd you run here?"

"Oh!" His smile took a more mischievous note. "I wanted to get here first to ask. Is Marii with anyone?"

They rushed downstairs to the grand hall where Marii and Peytire were placed to wait. Peytra burst through the doors to see the two still in awe of the grandness of it. Peytra and Georgie both seemed to notice how Marcus was coming into the hall from a side entrance to see the commotion, but before he could approach either of the newcomers, Peytra and Marii ran into each other's arms. Peytire quickly joined the two exclaiming sisters, picked up and spun Peytra.

"Look at our baby beastie! Don't look like a lady of the house yet!" said Peytire, pulling Peytra in under his shoulder.

"Oy! Petie! Stop!" Peytra whined as he ruffled her hair.

"Well, he's not wrong! Look at you, soon-to-be Duchess or some such and still wearing working frocks!" Marii said, tugging at the brown over-frock that Peytra preferred to wear when running around the castle. Looking up at Marii, she could see how Georgie could be so stricken with her so soon. She was more beautiful than Peytra remembered. Her golden hair having grown out a bit since she'd last seen her, and her skin still sun-kissed from the fall, Marii was like a walking sunray.

"Well, maybe it was all an elaborate joke, eh, Mar? Our little beastie couldn't be marrying a duke."

"I am too!" And like that, Peytra was back to her former self, tussling with her siblings as she pinched Peytire's side. All three of them began to play fight and were only interrupted by a polite cough. They turned towards the noise, and there was the Duke, flanked by Hue and Una. Peytra could see the smile lines in his eyes and knew that he was having a good private chuckle. She was dismayed at her siblings, however, who sobered and had terribly stoic expressions on their faces. Fear, she realized. What they had was fear for his masked appearance. Her heart broke a little in response.

"Your Grace," said Marii, with her eyes downturned, and curtsied. She elbowed Peytire, who followed suit.

Peytra felt the need to quell their fear and prove that yes, she was engaged to him. "Jors." She walked to him and grabbed a gloved hand. "This is my sister Marii and my brother Peytire."

"Nice to finally meet you. Peytra has told me much about you."

Peytra was silently amazed at how Marii's face could pale and blush at the exact same time.

"It seems they've come for a surprise visit," Peytra said.

"Well, not surprise exactly," interjected Una, and she tilted her head to face Peytra. "His Grace felt that you may have had some homesickness and asked me to write to your family."

"That's right," Peytire said, keeping his composure, but leveling his suspicious gaze on the frightening masked presence that held his sister's hand. "Da and Ma wanted to come, but Da's so busy with all the new orders, we came ahead."

"And I'm glad of it," said Jors. "I also believe we've made room arrangements."

"Well…they did come early," Una mumbled. "I'll handle it." She turned around with Hue on her footsteps. They grabbed Marcus by each of his arms on the way out, stating something about needing help, but it was clear that they saw the way Marcus looked at her siblings and wanted to give them a breath before they had to deal with his advances.

"So," Peytire said, straightening up, his eyes glaring directly at the Duke, "you're marrying my baby sister?"

If Jors was taken aback by the shift in Peytire's voice he didn't show it. "It would seem so." He ran his thumb gently over her knuckle.

"Well, what I want to know is why didn't you ask for our father's permission? Nor did you introduce yourself to the family before doing so."

At this, Jors did shift his stance. "I was not aware

that a grown woman needed permission to marry whomever she pleased." Peytra could see a small, satisfied smirk working its way on Marii's face. "As for my introduction to your family, I did meet your parents briefly and was graced by their kindness. I am trying to rectify any other impressions now by inviting you all to our home."

Peytra tried not to look struck by the word. *Our.* The castle, which was her home, was both of theirs.

Peytire calmed for a moment, considering this man. Then walked up to the Duke and wrapped his arms around him. Peytra couldn't read Jors' face, but she easily guessed it was one of shock. "Well then! Welcome to the family, brother!" And he proceeded to lift the Duke off the ground. Peytra caught Peytire's mischievous wink and held back a laugh.

She playfully smacked her brother's arm after he put down the Duke. "Stop trying to frighten my future husband!"

Peytire let the man go and pretended to look admonished. "Well, it would have been better if Thom and Lukas could make it..." Peytra pictured her oldest brothers, their imposing height and reddish-gold beards, bearing down on Jors. She hid her laugh behind a forced cough.

Marii went over to Peytra's side and grabbed her hand the way she did when they were little, and Marii would drag Peytra's over to their neighbor's to play. "So. Are my sister and her new betrothed going to give me a tour of their home, or am I going to have to wait until I get lost?"

"Oy, but can we stop at our rooms first? These bags are going to rip my shoulder off," said Peytire, dramatically lifting their packs.

The foursome did go to the rooms first on the opposite wing of the castle. They were quickly shooed away by the flurry of staff readying the rooms. They took themselves out to the gardens, even though the ground was cold with the touch of early winter. They snuck into the kitchen, where Gani was not having the group there to distract everyone as they prepared for the dinner rush. She did allow them to take a few items to graze on, but no more than a half-loaf and some fruit and cheese, or they were to have their fingers crushed by her rolling pin.

They then went to the hallway that Peytra's archways adorned. Marii and Peytire were all too happy to offer their semi-professional opinions on her work. Growing up with their father meant they all had a familiarity with carving and sculpture, which they wielded on one another with the kind of casual criticism that is only bred in siblinghood.

"You know, if you'd have used a pointed knife to do the gouging on that filigree work instead of a small chisel, you would have gotten a nice rounded shape to the dots on those leaves," said Marii, a hand on her chin.

"Yeah, but it's harder to control for depth if you hammer in at a straight angle with a pointer; I have more control with an angled chisel," Peytra replied, trying not to sound irked.

"Just use a measuring block."

"That doesn't work when you're moving in different depths on the carving. Besides, I wanted the darkened portions to have a certain roughness. Really play with how the contrast looks in light and shadow," Peytra said while straightening up, confident in her creative decisions.

"You know…" Peytire squinted his eyes and tilted his head, "if you had just moved those two figures up half a finger-length, you could have made a really nice triangle shape with the figures."

Peytra looked upwards, "Fregh's collar! You're right! How did I miss that?" Peytra began mentally calculating ways she could modify it. *Maybe I can move the others down? Supplement some areas with clay? But then the materials wouldn't mesh…*

Jors put a comforting hand on her shoulder. "I think they're perfect as is. And besides, it's more impressive to keep the figures in frame like that."

Peytra absentmindedly laid her hand on his hand at her shoulder. She felt calm wash over her. She hadn't realized how much she needed him for comfort until now.

They took a break to eat an informal dinner, except Jors, who ate in the privacy of his rooms but came down soon after. The siblings spent time regaling the others with stories of their little village and Peytra's youth. They told tales of how the three of them, the youngest and most likely to be left to their own devices, would cause all sorts of mischief. They talked about how they'd steal all the apples from their mother's storage, eat them, and leave only the cores. Or of the time they each tried to get the neighbor's mute cow to moo by dancing and making ridiculous faces at it. They told a story of how they stole every left shoe from their siblings and parents and hid them at the top of a tree. Not wanting to be obvious, they also hid their own left shoes. They laughed uncontrollably when it was discovered because a bird had built its nest in their father's old boot.

"You should have seen his face when he saw that sparrow in there! He kept trying to move it, and the sparrow would swoop down and almost peck his eye out!" said Marii

"Remember what he said when he got tired of trying to win his shoe back? 'Eh! It's for the birds! It was an old shoe anyway!'" said Peytire, swinging his arms in perfect imitation of their father.

Peytra stopped her laughing to interject, "He was furious with us! How'd you come up with that idea?"

"Me?" said Peytire, pointing to himself. "It was Marii's idea!"

"No, it wasn't!" said Marii, indignant. "It was yours!" She pointed to Peytra.

"No! I remember! It was Marii's! You came up with it after Ma told us story of the maiden with the cursed shoes! You said, 'Well, let's make sure no one get's cursed!'"

"Really? No… Really?" said Marii.

"Yes! But I don't remember why we just took left shoes," said Peytra

"I think it was because I don't like the word 'left.' It's a bit awkward to say. Left. Lefftuh," Marii said, straining the word with her tongue.

"But why only one shoe?" said Kori.

"Oh, that's 'cause little beastie here said that if one foot should get cold, we wouldn't want the other to," Peytire answered with a smile.

"Why do you call her 'beastie'?" asked Hue, an unreadable expression on his face.

"'Cause right when she was born, she was scarcely still a little babe. Peytire had never really seen a baby before up close. I remember she was all still in a bundle when Ma and Pa told us she would be our new sister. And Peytire here tried to poke her cheek with his finger. Well, it must have spooked her because she turned her wee baby head and bit straight down on his finger. Hard," said Marii

"Oy! It hurt! I still have the scar!" He pointed to his index finger at the almost invisible mark.

"He ran around the whole house screaming,

'She's a beast! She's gonna eat me!' dripping blood everywhere," Marii said with a chuckle.

Peytra leaned back and crossed her arms, a smug look crossing her face, "Well, he shouldn't have poked me!"

"Once a beastie, always a beastie," Peytire said while wiggling his index finger near her cheek. She suddenly snapped her jaws close to it, and it surprised him so much he fell backwards off his chair. They all erupted into laughter as Marcus helped lift him back up.

Somehow the conversation turned to Peytra's soon to be position in the household and all that it entailed. Which even Peytra wasn't so sure about.

"It's, well, it's not easy to describe what a Duchess does. My mother was never crowned a Duchess because she had no known parentage. And I do not have the chance to meet with women of my exact station," said Jors, with a pleading look to Una to elaborate.

Una coughed, "It's – Well – From my readings on the matter, a Duchess' main duties are to produce heirs. After that, it's really dependent on the needs of the Dukedom, and whether the title was inherited patrilineally or matrilineally. From what I gather, they can do as much as a duke is expected or less. It's really not fully specified."

"I worked with the Duke of Calmantic a few years back," said Georgie. "The Duchess seemed to be most concerned by giving grand parties. But then, it was a loveless marriage. I could see wanting that distraction."

"Oh, I remember that, but then again, the Duke of Calmantic did not have the same hands-on rule that His Grace does. It was rumored he gambled most of the money earned by his properties away every season. His group of advisers and counselors could do nothing to stop it," Hue piped in.

Peytra had paled. "Heirs?"

Jors had a sudden panicked look in his eyes, "Not right away! Not at all if you don't want to!"

"I was just, caught off guard," she said, letting out the tension. They'd had the conversation. Neither was prepared for children, although they both wanted children, eventually. She had to remember to procure pickled fennel to avoid an unexpected pregnancy. It was becoming ever harder to resist one another when their passions for each other were creeping higher and higher. She tried to contain her flush by stuffing herself with a spare sweetened bread slice.

The topic quickly shifted away from her responsibilities and heir-bearing to what a Duchess would wear and have. It then led to a conversation about her new quarters, which Marii demanded to see immediately. Peytire seconded the motion, and somehow the entire party trekked upstairs to her room. Gani forcing Georgie and Peytire to carry a giant pot of warmed, liquid crème and chocolate, Hue bringing a pot of mulled wine, Kori bringing a stack of sweets while Hue was loaded with mugs. The party entered her room, already lit by Peytra's probably sleeping handmaid, and she got to experience the wonder of the space all over again through fresh eyes.

As Gani prepared the hot drink, Georgie and Hue poured out the mulled wine, and Marii ran through every cabinet Peytra now had. Her bureaus and armoires were still mostly empty because she'd been lax in adding to her Ducal wardrobe. That was something Marcus was all too happy to point out. Peytra couldn't help but blush at Marii's wonder as she examined the murals, the architecture, the grandness of it all. She perused and shrieked at Peytra's small collection of new gowns, fingering the fine material and colors. Marii ran around Peytra's office, complementing the furniture while still scolding her for having such a mess.

Peytire snuck up next to Peytra's side and put an arm around her shoulder while Marii was squealing over a wall sconce. "So, Beastie, even without all this, are you happy?"

She looked up at his searching and concerned face. Her eyes traveled around the room. There were Gani and Kori, arms around each other's waists. Gani sipped at her cup, and Kori's hand played absentmindedly with her lover's hair. They were both listening to Georgie's story about some such adventure, his smile brightening his roundish face. Una and Hue sipped their mulled wine face to face, in some intimate flirtation. Her smile turned girlish in response to his. There was Marii, now being told some history of a painting in the room by Marcus, her hand on her chin in intense concentration, and Marcus putting forth his most charismatic instructional voice.

Then she looked to Jors, her soon-to-be husband as he sat on a low couch. His sitting posture relaxed as he chuckled to something Georgie had said. She remembered how he'd seemed so reserved when they first met. Now he sat casually among the group of them, his laugh a warm blanket that floated from the heart to her ear. Even from their distance, she could see his bright blue eyes as they met hers. Every time he looked at her like that, a buzzing feeling hit her stomach. He was her home. She smiled.

"Yes, I'm very happy," and she looked up at her brother. He smiled back.

The rest of the evening was spent cavorting around the fire. One by one or pair by pair, the visitors trickled out of her quarters. Until well into the night, it was simply her and Jors sitting in front of the fire. They gazed at the embers in silence, in much the way they did that first night in his study. Peytra took in a deep breath, absorbing the scent of the fire and of him.

"Thank you." She turned her face to smile at him. His gaze was questioning. "Thank you for inviting my family. I needed it."

"Well, you'd been quite stressed and out of sorts, and I had to remember you'd grown up with brothers and sisters. It seemed natural that they would be the best people to know what you needed," he said, running a gloved hand through her hair. "And besides, I needed to get to know my future in-laws."

"Ah? And your impressions?"

"I sense a trap." If she could've seen his face, she would have sworn that he was raising an eyebrow.

She playfully pushed her shoulder against him. "Really."

"Well, I would say, in all honesty, that they are quite wonderful. And that you are very lucky to have them in your life and that I may be the luckier one by marrying into that."

"I think Marcus may be missing his gilded tongue."

"Marcus better not have left his tongue in here."

Peytra laughed, a deep and unrestrained joyful noise coming forth. He pulled her into his shoulder, and she rested a hand on his thigh. "But truly, do you like them?"

"Honestly? I love them. They are a part of who

you are, and they love you too. I couldn't help but love them."

She smiled into his shoulder as her fingers drew careless circles on his thigh. "Do you sometimes wish you had siblings?"

He was silent for a time, eyes transfixed in the hearth for several measured heartbeats. Peytra worried she had struck a nerve. Then he swallowed and answered, "While I was a very young child, I did not. I remember being frightened by the prospect that my mother's attention would go to someone else. Then when she left, I remember wishing that there were others there to share in my father's wrath, that I did not take on all of it. When my father died, I cursed that I never had an older brother to take on the responsibilities of a dukedom. I resented that I had been born alone then.

"To be fair, I had a type of siblinghood. Marcus has been with me, and we love and fight like brothers. I've often felt that Elle was a sort of sister, and Gani as well. But now I am overjoyed to be marrying into a family like yours."

She nuzzled closer to him, listening to the steady thump of his heartbeat. Content with the intimacy, she kept running her fingers along his thigh, climbing ever higher. "And I'm happy to be marrying you."

He ran his hand down her back. "Truly?"

"Yes," she said, her voice an earnest whisper. They sat like that in silence interrupted only by the low crackling in the hearth. Her thoughts were adrift, leaving her mind wordless, but replaced with her slowly building vivid imagery. She noted the taut muscle in his thigh and thought about the body that must be below that thick woolen layer. Her head was cradled against a firm pectoral, and she reminisced over how her hands would glide over his chest at night. She wanted to see him, at least some part of him in those moments of tender passion. An idea slowly began to take hold.

Her fingers played along the inside of his thigh, coming up to the bulge in between. She took her index finger and slowly traced it, noting his sharp intake in breath. Then, she took her entire palm and applied pressure moving upwards. "Peytra…" he growled. She loved the sound. She pushed her breasts against him and stroked once more.

"Jors," she said, her voice growing husky with desire. She stroked again and brought her other hand forward to begin unbuttoning her dress.

"Get the blindfold," he almost commanded her, his need growing with every touch.

"No. Not yet," she said. With one last stroke, she stood up and took off her dress. She slowly drew off her slip and stood nude in front of him. Her eyes followed his gaze, and it assessed her. All of her. She could read that look of hunger, of affection, of love and appreciation. It emboldened her to go forth with her next step. She laid down on rug in front of the fire, the light highlighting her curved form in the darkness. Shadows shortened and expanded beneath her breasts as she breathed. Watching him, she glided one hand downwards towards the region between her thighs. She took one finger and began to massage her clitoris in small circles.

Jors sat enthralled in his seat, a hand moving to his swollen penis to mimic the motions she had done before. She watched him move, and with each pass of her finger, movements built up speed. Her breaths became shallow and rapid as she held his gaze, her body growing more and more tense from the buildup.

Jors left his seat and kneeled next to her. His

gloved hands explored her body as she pleasured herself. The nearness of him, the steady craving in his gaze, and the ever-faster way she stimulated herself brought her to the brink of climax. Normally she would have closed her eyes, but this time she refused. She wanted to at least see some part of him. As she felt her thighs tense and her toes curl, she took her free hand and rubbed Jor's penis over his clothing. He let out a groan of pleasure but returned to touching her, eyes locking with her at the moment that she climaxed. He put his hand over the hand that was massaging her clitoris and applied a little more pressure to make the orgasm last. She slowed her movements and collapsed against the rug.

Jors effortlessly picked her up from the ground and walked her over to her bed. The coolness of the soft sheets sent a chill through her. He lovingly tied her blindfold before throwing off his mask and kissing her deeply. One hand clasped her by the back of the neck to keep the kiss in place, while his other hand went to undoing his doublet. Her hands, guided by need and instinct, helped him to strip away his covering, then his pants. Jors pushed off his boots and crawled onto the bed.

He hovered over her form, his eyes roving and taking in her body. The beginnings of winter led the castle to always have a slight draft, but both their bodies exerted such a heat that they glistened from the sweat. In the low light, he could see how the outline of her body curved in on itself just above her hip. He took his right hand and ran it from her nape to her collar bone, down her breast and stomach to reach between her thighs.

She was still sensitive from her previous orgasm, and when his middle finger just brushed her clitoris, she writhed and moaned in a pleasurable shock. An unseen smile lit up Jor's face. This is what he wanted, for his touch to give her joy. He began to mimic her earlier movements with slow circles. Already close to the edge, her next climax came quickly. Her body arched off the bed, breasts falling to her sides. She collapsed into the sheets gasping for the cold air to still her body that shook with the current of the orgasm.

But he was still filled with hunger.

He tilted her body onto its side and raised her leg. He tilted his head in between her thighs and put his tongue to work. What he did not consider was that, at this upside-down angle, he would be vulnerable to her need to pleasure him. She grasped his penis with both hands and put her mouth on it. He paused from the sudden sensation to gasp, and that only motivated her. They continued, devouring each other in competition. Each, claiming a minor victory, had to pause in their action to take in the sensation.

When she climaxed, he could feel the vibration on his tongue and through hers. She took one final swallow leading him to climax. They clung to each other in the sweet closeness and exhaustion. He crawled up to her and held her shuddering body to him. In the freezing night, the two lovers clung to one another, taking solace in the heat of the body that lay next to them.

CHAPTER 14

Winter was now a full-fledged season. Snow left the ground unusable, but Peytra and Jors still found themselves outdoors on their daily strolls. Marii and Peytire had taken over much of the wedding decision-making. This was not as arduous a task as first thought. Even though the nobility from near and far had been invited, few felt the urgency to leave the warmth of their walls to travel to stand on some ceremony. There was a steady flow of polite declines to their invitation. That suited the betrothed all too well, who would have preferred to have a small ceremony all to themselves.

The only guests to arrive were the small circle of Jors' closest noble friends and Peytra's family and family friends. Elle had arrived in the past week with her guest, the Lady Antel, whom Peytra remembered from the masque. Marii and the Baroness were fast friends and already plotting all sorts of holidays that they could all venture on. In the meantime, Peytire and Marcus were often off on their own. They'd become companions, and perhaps, Peytra suspected, something more. There was more than one occasion when she'd accidentally walked in on them in a moment of quiet conversation. Sometimes they seemed to be sharing intimate thoughts or secrets; other times, it was more intense and urgent. Either way, both seemed to have a relaxed presence around the other. They seemed calmer, happier. Peytire had a quiet brightness about him that she'd never noted until now.

This, however, did not prevent them from causing trouble. There was a day where both Peytra and Marii were busy with other matters and thus ignored Peytire and Marcus. The duo found themselves with not much to do while a snowstorm raged outdoors and so concocted a plan to "replace" the two women. Their replacements came in the form of two old mops dressed in old frocks that they paraded around the castle and addressed as Peytra and Marii. This joke came to a head at dinner where the mops were seated at the table, and the rest of the joking bunch got in on the act, ignoring the physical versions in favor of the parody.

At one point, Jors even turned to the mop and said very earnestly, "How are you enjoying tonight's soup, my dear?" which led to a red-faced and laughing Peytire.

The women got their vengeance by taking the mops and puppetting them. They began to use their mops to chase the group around the dinner table and made mocking impressions of themselves and others. The prank only stopped when people were laughing so hard they could scarcely breathe. They all collapsed in their seats, heaving.

Peytra walked with her hand in the crook of Jors' arm and reflected on these days of joy. Her parents were to arrive the following day or the day after, and then in another day's time, she and Jors would be married. While the thought of being a duchess, or a wife, or rather the thought of being anything other than the simple carver she'd always considered herself to be filled her with a certain queasiness, she was happy. This castle was her own little island away from everything. Jors, with his even-tempered nature, his sensitivity and hushed passion, was her solace.

Yet, the curiosity still dug at her. Most of the time, Peytra didn't even remember that she'd never seen him. Her mind substituted that dream version she had of him in her memories. A dream version that seemed to make more and more appearances. In her dreams, he was the same Jors, the same sound to his voice, the same cadence to his walk, but his face was growing ever more manic. He was desperate, he said. He was searching for a way to break the curse that kept them from one another. He begged her to trust him. To be patient and to love him. She already did.

When those dreams ended with him clawing at himself, shrieking about the things on his skin, she would wake up gasping and in a cold sweat. She'd sometimes forget that she had a blindfold and would fear that she'd gone blind. Jors would be there, his body marked by the sweat of a nightmare, and he would hold her, soothe her until she fell back asleep.

These dreams weren't helped by the late hours that Jors was keeping with that old question he was trying to solve. He'd stay late in the night in his study, reading and translating. And while he always made it to bed, it would be well after Peytra had already dozed off. She was beginning to suspect that Otik, the dream dealer, was playing a cruel trick on her and perhaps giving her Jors' nightmares. When she thought of it that way, though, that she was taking on whatever would bother Jors, it calmed her. She'd gladly take on whatever was ailing him, but she wanted a full night's sleep.

"What's on your mind?" Jors said, picking her out of her silent revelry.

"Just thinking about Otik." It was true.

"The dream giver?"

"Giver? I'd always heard him as the dream 'dealer.'" Peytra wasn't quite sure, but that distinction seemed important for some reason.

"Dealer? No, Otik gives dreams to those who need them. Sometimes to inspire, sometimes to give forewarnings," said Jors with a very assured tone.

Peytra was irked by his surety. "No, he deals out dreams AND nightmares. He deals them out on a whim, and you must appease him for a good dream. Sometimes he gets drunk on the Gods' wine and switches dreams, which leads to false prophecy."

Jors shook his head. "Otik gives dreams, his twin brother Kjink gives nightmares, and their sister, Ingle, gives messages of prophecy. They are the children on Enting, the East wind."

The name Ingle did seem familiar, but she remembered Ingle as a witch who spoke lies and was tied face-first to a tree for it. She wondered why she had heard a story like that in school. She also had the notion that Jors was generally right about these things. He'd grown up surrounded by books and records. Her knowledge of the finer points of their religion came by word of mouth, passed down again and again in such a way that they may not reflect them as they were first.

However, she also wanted to win the argument. "Enting has never had children!"

Jors chuckled. "Let's ask Marcus."

They found Marcus and Peytire in the library, engaged in some sort of comical conversation, but they brightened on seeing the other two enter.

"Marcus."

"Yes, Your Grace." Marcus made a dramatic bow, and Peytra didn't have to look to know that Jors was rolling his eyes.

"Might you settle an argument for us?" said Jors.

"Ah, and what might the happy couple be arguing about that I would dare to get in the middle of?" Marcus said with a wry half-smile scrolling its way across his face.

"We'd like to know the names of Enting's first children."

At that moment, Peytra saw Marcus do something she thought him incapable of: he blushed. Not only that, he sobered his features in such a way that Peytra barely recognized him. Peytire, Peytra, and even Jors all went silent, uncomfortable in the presence of a darkened Marcus.

Marcus swallowed and then looked Jors directly in the eye. "You know names have power. I make no apologies." He closed his eyes, and upon opening them, a false smile was plastered on his face like a child's incongruous graffiti. "Well, Enting had several children. The most well-known are the triplets who —" As Marcus was walking towards a shelf to pick out a book, they were interrupted by Una and Kori.

"Your Grace, there is a messenger from the King. Would you like to meet him?" Una said.

Jors took a deep, frustrated breath. "Yes," he turned to Peytra, "I'll be right back, please let me know how right I was when I return."

She could detect the playful smile beneath the mask and gave him a push on the way out. Kori lingered by the door. "What are you all doing?" she asked, stepping into the room.

"Oh, just settling an argument," said Peytra. "Jors believes there are three gods of dreams. Otik, Kjink, and Ingle."

What followed was a situation that Peytra would deny ever happened to herself for days after. She rationalized it as a bout of dizziness or a poor spot of porridge. Or the constant restlessness and nightmares. The instance frightened her such that she did her best to bury the memory, only to have the words repeat themselves over and over again.

All the lights in the room went out in one gust of Eastward wind. The temperature dropped as if the windows had been shattered, but it was only an illusion. The lights re-lit a second later, but when they did, Peytire, Marcus, and Kori had their heads bent forward, their figures lined up in a triangle formation in front of Peytra.

Marcus took a sudden, deep breath, and his face cracked upwards. When he opened his eyes, they glowed an otherworldly blue. "Well, well, well," he said, a voice that was and was not Marcus's came out of the mouth. It was the timbre of Marcus's voice, but it had the echo of another. He examined his hands and felt at his face.

Peytire followed suit, his eyes with a deep purple glow. Peytire's face, which usually glowed with a boyish joy, was now set in a haunted formation. Kori did the same, her eyes glowing gold. Her face took on an ageless quality.

Kori's voice rang out like a bell at midnight, foreboding. "Ah, you are in little brother. He will not be happy about that, Otik."

The Marcus-that-was-not-Marcus answered, "No. I suspect not Ingle. But I'm his favorite sibling. I send him good dreams on his birthday." Otik's haughty sneer almost looked familiar.

"Ha! You don't even know when his birthday is!" the violet-eyed Peytire scoffed.

"Oh yes I do, Kjink!" said Otik

"Oh yeah? When is it then?"

"It's... it's in the Winter..." Otik scratched the borrowed nose to Kjink's haughty expression. "You just want me to tell you because you forgot!"

"Will you two please stop your bickering for once!" said Ingle, pushing Kori's braid from her shoulder to let it hang along her back. "You two are the reason he never lets us visit!"

"Baby brother is really going to hate you for using his body," Kjink laughed.

"This isn't my doing! I don't know why we're here." Otik turned to Ingle. "Care to shed some light on the situation, sister?"

"Yes. I have a message for the girl." They all turned to look at Peytra, who was seated petrified on a tufted ottoman. She felt like holding her breath and closing her eyes until they all went away. But her curiosity got the best of her. She'd heard tales of the gods using the bodies of mortals before, but she never thought those tales quite so literal. Then there was the way they kept referring to Marcus as "brother," but that would mean.... No. She refused to even draw that conclusion. The idea of Marcus being a god was laughable! She would have laughed, were she not so terrified.

"Couldn't you have just visited her in her sleep like you do the others? And why did we all have to come?" said Kjink.

"I was not able to get into her dreams. Another one has been speaking to her. Besides, the wards brother has placed are too strong for my ordinary power," Ingle answered.

"Yes, but why, dear sister, do we all have to be here?" said Otik

"Just a coincidence. We were all called. Besides, aren't you happy to see little brother?"

"I can't very well see him if I'm in him!" screeched Otik.

"And I doubt he'll ever let you see him now that you've desecrated his form with your presence." Kjink's glee was apparent.

"And you? You're in the body of his lover. I doubt he'll appreciate that very much," Otik said to Kjink, his face now taking on Marcus's characteristic mischief. Kjink's dawning realization played a frown on Peytre's face.

"My goodness, I cannot take you two anywhere! Let me deliver the message, and we can be gone!" Ingle turned to Peytra and burrowed her golden eyes into Peytra. "You will have to make a choice. You can exist as it is or follow your desires. If you wish to break the curse, you must first set it off. But there is a risk and a price. Be prepared to pay it."

Peytra stared at the familiar face with the unfamiliar gaze. "Curse? What curse? What price? I don't understand."

"Listen to her when she tells you. Even when it hurts," said Ingle. Then, with a sudden snap of her fingers, everything went black.

When Peytra woke, she'd been moved to a nearby couch. Everything was hazy, but just then, Kori was running in with a maid and a cup of water. Peytire bent over her, and unsure if her brother was still possessed, she screamed!

"Oy beastie! I know I look a bit tired, but I didn't think I looked that horrible!" She looked to see if he retained any of that purple glow in his eyes. He did not, and thus began Peytra's denial of the events that took place.

"What happened?" she said, rubbing her forehead.

"You passed out suddenly," said Kori, "I've called for a doctor. We can take you to your rooms. How are you feeling?"

"I'm fine. I just – I guess I must be tired. Haven't been sleeping well," she answered.

"Well, best be taking you to your rooms." Peytire lifted her up into his arms the way he did when they were younger and she'd hurt her knee. While being carried out of the library, she turned and looked back to see Marcus, with an uncharacteristic stoic look, standing in the shadows and watching her.

Despite her protests, Peytra had been consigned to her bed for the rest of the day. The doctor had been interrupted during his afternoon meal and still had crumbs stuck to the front of her apron. She took a long look at Peytra and pronounced that, at the moment, she could find nothing wrong, but it would be better for her to remain in bed and rest for the remainder of the afternoon and evening.

Jors came as soon as he was notified, worried that something had befallen her, and had to be assured that yes, she was fine. He finished what business he had and returned to spend the day with her.

The remainder of the day was spent playing cards or reading with her fiancé, siblings, and friends piling into the giant bed. It was mostly Marii, Una, and Elle who would peek in from time to time. Elle was more than happy to introduce them to a game called "Houses" that she had picked up, and was all too happy to be the only experienced player in a game full of novices. She gleefully won the first two rounds. After Una played the second time, she seemed to get the skill for it. Her mathematical mind ended up being the key to the game, and she won the rest of the games.

Peytra enjoyed the time with her friends and welcomed the distraction. Normally she was an active worker and would have loathed spending her time like this with her feet up. But after that afternoon's scene, she wanted to do anything to take her mind off her hallucination. And she most certainly did not wish to be alone. As the hours whiled away and people drifted to their beds and Jors felt the need to do more of his research, it came to be that it was just Marii as the night became late.

In a moment of silence, as both nursed a hot chocolate while the snow was a steady stream on the window, Marii took a sip from her mug and looking down at the liquid. "Peytra, you – you didn't faint because you're with child, did you?"

Peytra almost spit her hot chocolate all over the bed. "No! No. I've been eating a pickled fennel every day! And besides..." She was unsure how much she wanted to divulge her bedroom activities to her sister.

"Oh! So you two have been together!" Marii had an open-mouthed smile that pushed her high cheeks into her eyes. "Tell me, just between us, what does he look like underneath all that?" She waved a hand in front of her face.

"I wouldn't know," said Peytra remorsefully, looking into her mug. Something tugged at the back of her mind. She ignored it.

"How do you not? You're about to get married! And you've been together..."

"Well, it's, there's a blindfold. And not simply

that, I trust him. He trusts me. And he doesn't want me to see his burned body."

"Have you told him this?"

"Yes! But he just, he just needs more time." That feeling that had been eating at her was now coming forward. She couldn't rectify his need for privacy, his fear of her gaze with his love. She wished he would have faith in her to know that, no matter how horribly burnt he may be, she would love him.

"Well, you have more patience than I have, sister. I don't think I could live like that. The curiosity would kill me." Marii took a long sip of her drink.

"I really have no choice. He won't show me, and I've asked."

"Then again, he doesn't have to know," said Marii with a secretive look in her eyes. Peytra raised an eyebrow. Marii continued. "It's simple, really, just wait until he's asleep and then light a candle and look at him. He won't have to know that you know."

It was as if an arrow had gone through her, piercing the softest end of her heart. What had she heard earlier? About following her words? Everything ached in her. It would be a simple solution, and yet, it picked at their trust. "What if he figures out that I did that? What if he finds out I know?"

"You could wait until after you're wed. That way, it wouldn't be as if you're looking for an easy escape. And then he would know that you still committed to the marriage. You'll also get to know what your husband looks like."

That feeling tugged at Peytra and the hazy memory of the warning she was trying to forget. "I don't know…"

"You don't have to do it or even tell me if you've done it. I'm just giving you an idea in case you ever have the need." She patted Peytra's arm. But the tug never quite left.

That night, when Jors came to bed, she held onto him and kissed him like it was the first and last time. She needed to remember her love and try to assuage the guilt she felt for the way she planned to betray his trust.

CHAPTER 15

The morning of her wedding dawned, and Peytra was in a haze. The rest of her family had arrived two days before, and that alone had kept her occupied and distracted enough not to think about the things that had happened or were about to.

Her sisters, mother, Kori, and her maid now dominated her rooms and took turns fussing over her hair, face paint, and gown. She wore a golden thing with deep chestnut chevrons in the trim. Her waist was accented with a deep red iftink, the wedding belt. This iftink was embellished with gold embroidery. She dawned a red juntok for what would be the walk to the temple. It hooked to her shoulders with a hidden clasp. While her mother attached the juntok, she told Peytra of how she felt on her wedding day. Her father had lost his iftink clipping that morning and ran around through his workshop. Ottoh had actually located the clipping next to the wedding gift he was to give her, but by that point, they were all late to the temple.

"My mother was fuming!" said Peytra's mother as she straightened the cape. "She screamed at your father for a good few minutes because she thought he was trying to get out of the marriage."

"I thought Mamit loved Father?" asked Peytra, absentmindedly trying to keep with the conversation.

Her mother patted her shoulder. "She did! She was nervous since my first betrothal did not work out."

"You were engaged to someone else?" Marii chimed in, shocked.

"Oh yes, he was also a young guardsman with a penchant to flirtation. But when it came time to begin preparations, he broke off the engagement."

"I'm sorry, Mother," said Peytra, reaching over her shoulder and giving her mother's hand a squeeze. "I'm very happy you ended up with Father, though."

"I am too," said her mother. "That was a long time and many heartbreaks ago. And I couldn't be happier than I am now."

"Who was more handsome, though? Da or this beau?" said Marii, mischief apparent in her smile.

"If your father ever asks, it's him." Then her stern expression softened. "Yet if you were to ask my sisters at the time… well."

The women shook with laughter. Peytra managed a small chuckle as she examined herself in the mirror. Her image was unfamiliar with all this face painting and her hair put up in an ornate coiffure. She was pretty, but in a way that was unfamiliar to herself. She looked at the gown, it's low decolletage, which everyone insisted was in fashion, pushed her breasts into a slightly uncomfortable shape. The gold of it brought out the golden tones in her brown skin. Looking at the deep red juntok, iftink, and the rouge on her lips, she remembered what Jors had said: "Red really is your color."

What would he think when he saw her? A blush warmed her cheeks. She imagined that he would give her the same amorous look that he did when he wished to explore her body. It was a look she had yet to tire of. She looked forward to the ending of the ceremony, the end of their reception when they could simply be with one another. When she remembered what she planned to do after he fell asleep, the little flame of excitement wavered.

It was time, and the rest of Peytra's day went by in a haze. She remembered entering the temple. She remembered that her siblings had lined themselves up by age. Lukas stuck out his tongue at her in playful banter. Ottoh began crying even before her parents did. She remembered how the mask that Jors wore in the temple, the one she had made, seemed to move in the candlelight. There was the way his eyes locked on hers, blue meeting brown. He was smiling behind the visage, and she could tell by the way her cheeks burned that she was too. The priestess said some words, but she could not recall them. Instead, Peytra watched his eyes in front of the altar.

She remembered the smell of the smoke in the fire bowl after they made their offerings to the gods. They each took a pre-cut clipping from their iftinks and tossed them into the bowl. Each took a match and lit them on fire. This symbolized their union. Two burning as one flame. When Peytra looked in that bowl, its flames licking the edge, she could have sworn she'd seen a woman with red hair looking back at her.

She remembered walking into the reception hall, to the grand feast that Gani had meticulously planned and executed. She did not remember what she ate, only that she was full from the extravagance of it soon enough. Peytra recalled looking around the room to see her friends and family in revelry. Then there was a soft, gloved touch as Jors brushed a tear away. A tear of joy.

She remembered being announced as Duchess, but it would be a long time before she became comfortable with the title Jors had gifted her.

She remembered the way the music played and how she danced until her feet ached and her hair was coming undone. There was the way her brothers cornered Jors and lifted him over their heads to parade him around the hall. She could hear his deep, rich laugh from the other end, and she mirrored it in rhythm. Her heart was full, her life was full.

She remembered the celebratory champagne and how, starring into the drink, she wondered if it was possible to be this happy forever. Looking up, at the corner of her eye, she spied a red-haired woman who disappeared when Peytra turned around.

She remembered the slow trickle of guests retiring to their quarters. That the band played ever softer, lulling the revelers to their sleep.

She remembered how Jors took her hand and escorted her upstairs. Before getting undressed, they simply lay in bed, recounting the day. Jors mentioned how Marcus had done an entire speech about pleasing a woman in the early morning to anyone who would listen, and as a mock lecture to him. Una walked in on the exchange and roundly rebuffed that he had any such skill, which sent the whole group of them laughing. This sent Peytra laughing so hard that she nearly fell off the bed.

They talked about their friends, their family, the future. Then, as the hour got late, Jors had that look in his eye, where he seemed unable to peel his gaze away from her body. She stood up and undid her hair, letting it cascade behind her. Jors helped her undo her juntok, then her iftink. He undid his and gingerly wrapped one around the other and placed them on the nightstand. Peytra fiddled with her front lacing, but Jors made quick work of the front and back clasps. All the while, he ran his gloved hands along her sides, outlining her figure with his palms.

She stepped out of her gown and gently undid her slip. Naked, she stepped in between his legs where he sat on the bed. One hand touched his cowl and ran to his shoulder. The other hand brushed her fingers teasingly between his legs. She reached to the nightstand and grabbed the blindfold and tied it herself. She noted the position of the candle next to his bed.

After her blindfolding was complete, he blew out all the lights, so that he only had the light of the stars by which to guide him. He had memorized and loved every motion of her body. He undressed quickly, eager to feel her. When at last her body stood nude, warm against the cold, and his as well, he pulled her into a deep and all-encompassing kiss.

He pulled away. "Peytra…" he said, kissing her along her jaw, a hand pulling her toward him on the small of her back.

"Mmmm, yes, Jors?" Every hair on the back of her neck stood on edge at that touch of him.

"I love you." He kissed her collarbone.

She felt for his face. "I love you too." She kissed him deeply, tongues passing over each other with every sweet word they ever wished to whisper.

He lifted her up and placed her on the bed. With delicate maneuvering, he positioned himself above her. They kissed and tugged at one another, working each other into a passionate frenzy. He'd take a hand and play along her breasts and between her legs. She would take a hand and wrap it around his penis, pumping it to and fro. In retaliation, his hands went to work, moving at an ever-increasing pace. At a point, the pleasure became too great, and she grabbed the sheets at her sides, curled her toes, tightened her thighs and her breath until she shook with the pleasure of a climax.

He kissed her neck as she settled from it. "Peytra, may I…" he huffed. His body was burning with need, and she met it, heat for heat.

She knew what he wanted because she wanted it too. She bit at his neck and then whispered in his ear, "Jors, please, yes." She nibbled on his ear lobe, and he stilled his body. He sat up on his knees, carefully extricating himself from her embrace.

He looked at her, at all of her, at the woman he was to spend his life with, and noted how his arousal was only heightened by the love he had for her. Her flesh, her form, was perfect to him, but it was more than that. It was the way she smiled, the way she became absorbed in a project or her work. He could see her breathing hard in the starlight, and he wanted to bring her more pleasure. His fingers worked their way, massaging her clitoris lightly. While continuing that, he inserted his fingers one by one, noting what angles made her stomach twitch with excitement.

With a held breath, he guided himself toward her, and she moved her hips in return. As he pushed himself in, slowly, delicately, while massaging her clitoris, she moaned and huffed his name. She wrapped her legs around his waist to push him in further. He pushed in, and she sucked in her breath. She breathed him in, and for a moment, they were still. Peytra had never felt something like that, and she wanted to explore the feeling, the sensation of the two of them attached. He moved his hips, as did she.

They moved against one another, building speed. They clawed at each other, kissed and bit one another. Moaned one another's name. Peytra could feel the climax building, and she took sweet pleasure in the attachment. Hands grabbed at one another in the dark.

Blindfolded, every sensation was always an exciting shock. Now she felt the climax rush through her, the heat running from between her legs and spreading to the rest of her body. He climaxed as well, filling her with his heat. They trembled, and he lay down his body on her. They held each other, two bodies in the dark.

"Jors?" Peytra whispered, hours later. She said it again and felt to see he was there. Her hand ran down the center of his chest. He did not stir, though she could feel his breath on her skin. His chest heaved slowly as he slept. She whispered his name again. Confident enough that he would not wake if she moved, Peytra peeled off the blindfold. Her eyes took a moment to adjust. It was still dark, yet the moonlight from the high windows gave the room an eerie glow. Peytra did not remember the moon being full but thanked it for giving her enough light to fumble around.

She located a flint match on the nightstand and that candle from before. Stilling her hands, she took a few tries to light it. She paused while watching the small flame come to life. Peytra could turn back now if she wanted. All she would need to do was take a controlled breath and blow out the light, tie the blindfold, and go back to bed. Paralyzed with fear, she realized that the minute she turned around, she could never go back. Not that she would go back from her vows or choices, but that she could never go back to a time without this knowledge. Peytra had spent hours imagining what his burnt body must look like and found that she would still love him for it. But it was the knowledge of his image, tied with the betrayal of his trust that made her hesitate.

The minutes floated, and wax dripped and pooled near the wick. Peytra half hoped that the gods would prevent her from this choice by sending a breeze to blow out the light. But the air was still, and the gods were silent.

Grabbing the base of the candlestick, she closed her eyes and made her nerves calm themselves. Then she turned around slowly, the light illuminating the sheets in an orange circle. Then the light lit up the figure that had been sleeping next to her. Peytra gasped and covered her mouth at the sight of him.

He was not what she prepared for. Next to her was a body unburnt, unscarred. In fact, it was the man as she'd seen in her dreams. His reddish-blond hair made a mane around his sculpted face. His nose had a small crook to it, which only served to enhance how well-shaped the rest was. His chest was well-indented with muscle. Those arms that had held her so often, unsleeved, were firm and strong. She couldn't believe her eyes, and she began to cry, keeping her mouth covered to keep her as silent as possible.

But if he had not been maimed, why did he hide? She could not understand why someone so beautiful would cover every part of his body.

Then she saw it.

It moved and glided along the skin. It was a greenish-black mark that floated along the skin like a shadow gliding across the grass. It moved up the leg, and Peytra noted with horror that this was not some insect that could be shooed, it was part of him. It looked like two, illustrated eyes. When she bent closer to peer at it, it leapt from his skin to her face.

Peytra screamed, "Jors!" She could feel it clawing at her face, crawling its way to her eyes. In the panic, Peytra dropped the candle, and as Jors awoke, he was concerned with putting out the fire before his new wife was burnt. He did not notice right away that Peytra had put his curse in motion.

It took over her eyes. The thing dug into them, and it felt as if a hundred tiny needles were stabbing their way into her skull. It was an incredible, undeniable agony. For the briefest moment, her vision transported her to a room built into a cliff. She could see that it was night, through a window. But what she felt was much more sinister. It was desperation, it was cruelty.

When the curse had taken what was needed, it ripped itself away and flew out a westward window. Peytra screamed and felt at her face. Now that the small fire had been quelled, Jors grabbed her shoulders. His face moved from panic, to fear, to resolution.

"Peytra! Peytra! Listen to me!" He was breathing hard, his chest and shoulders quaking with the effort. Peytra stopped screaming, her breathing also labored. "Peytra! Listen! I'm so sorry I never could tell you! I wanted to tell you! I'm sorry! I love you. I love you." He took her into his arms and laid what felt like a kiss of finality. As she grasped to him, she could feel a pull. At first, she thought he was pushing himself from her embrace. But as the pull became stronger, she knew that he was holding on and that whatever was peeling him away was supernatural.

He was slipping away, and she held on. But he broke their kiss to grab her shoulders and look her in the eyes. "Peytra, my love. Let go." Her breath caught. She shook her head. "Peytra, my love, you have to let go." He had a small, resolute smile. A smile of goodbye. His hand came up and cupped her face, and he used his thumb to rub away a tear.

"I love you. I forgive you."

With that, her fingertips slipped, and he was swept from her in a supernatural wind. It sent him crashing through the window, shattering it and raining glass down like the falling snow. His body flew at incredible speeds, becoming a speck in the distance of a late-blooming dawn.

Peytra ran to the window, her feet cut on broken glass, but she did not care to feel it. When she spied out, she could see nothing but snow and the treetops, blurred in her tears.

Dear reader,

We hope you enjoyed reading *Mask of the Nobleman*. Please take a moment to leave a review, even if it's a short one. Your opinion is important to us.

Discover more books by Laura Diaz de Arce at

https://www.nextchapter.pub/authors/laura-diaz-de-arce

Want to know when one of our books is free or discounted? Join the newsletter at

http://eepurl.com/bqqB3H

Best regards,

Laura Diaz de Arce and the Next Chapter Team

ACKNOWLEDGMENTS

This began as a love letter to the little writer community which supported me in the beginning. So a hearty thank you goes to those who have accidentally lent their visage to their two-dimensional counterparts. Thank you Corrissa, Megan, Whiskey, Julia, Bedlam, J.D., Frawg, Gina, and Robert, I hope you like your fictional inspirations. As always, a thank you to my husband D.J., who is unconditionally supportive no matter the genre. Thanks to Mike Amato who has helped me stay grounded. Thanks to my parents, who I hope never read this because I do not want to discuss sex scenes with them.

Finally, all my love to you romantics. See you for the sequel!

ABOUT THE AUTHOR

Laura Diaz de Arce is a speculative author with a penchant for not sticking to one genre. She's the author of the short story collection *MONSTROSITY: Tales of Transformation*. Laura resides in a South Florida suburb with her husband and two cats. You can find her writings in many corners of the internet and her poorly curated presence on Twitter and Instagram @QuetaAuthor.

Mask Of The Nobleman
ISBN: 978-4-86745-745-0
Mass Market Paperback Edition

Published by
Next Chapter
1-60-20 Minami-Otsuka
170-0005 Toshima-Ku, Tokyo
+818035793528

29th April 2021

CPSIA information can be obtained
at www.ICGtesting.com
Printed in the USA
LVHW031125021021
699302LV00015B/1058